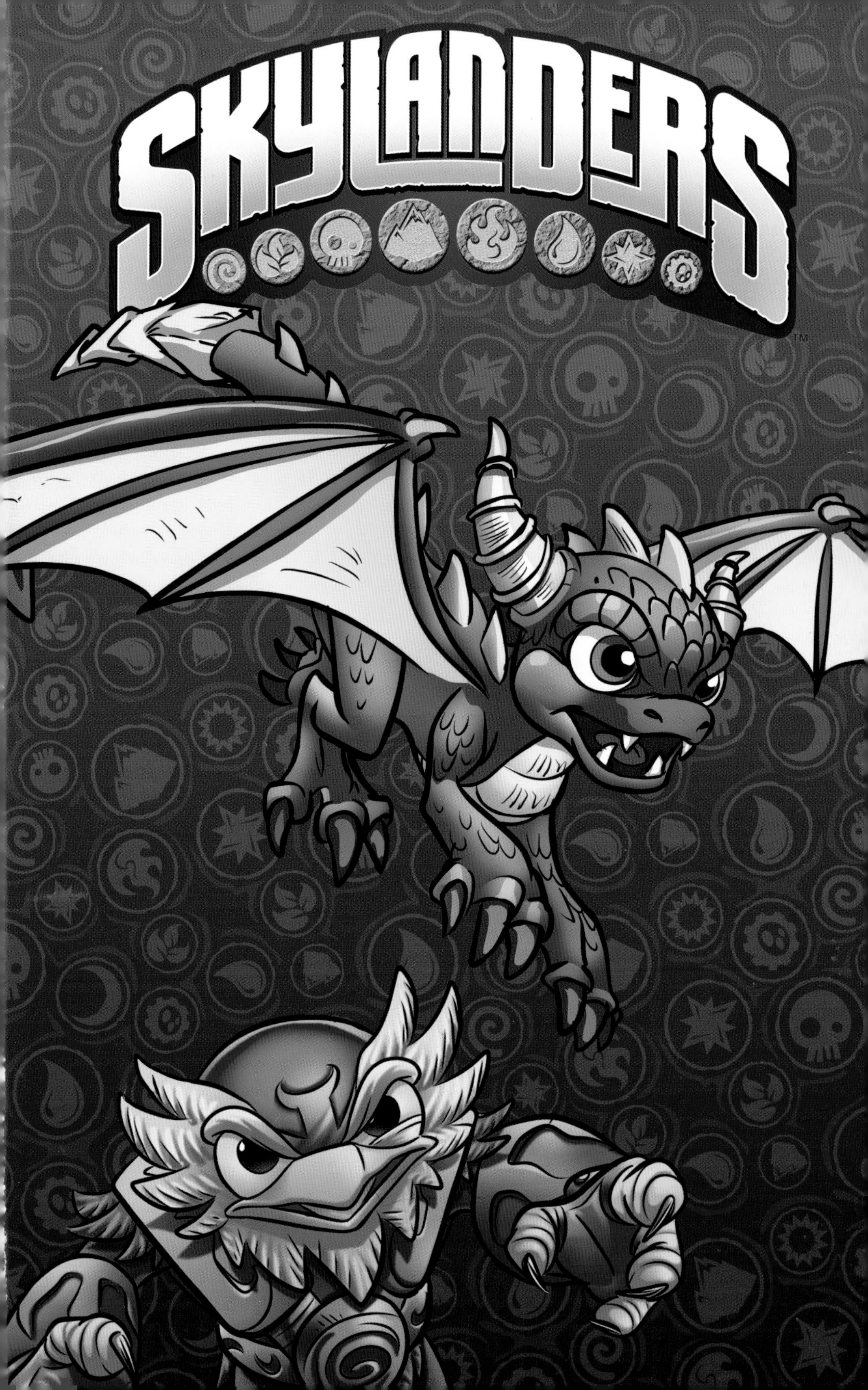
SKYLANDERS™

Cover Artist: **David Baldeon**
Cover Colorist: **David Garcia Cruz**
Series Edits: **David Hedgecock**
Collection Edits: **Justin Eisinger & Alonzo Simon**
Collection Designer: **Christa Miesner**
Publisher: **Ted Adams**

ISBN: **978-1-68405-128-1**

For international rights,
please contact licensing@idwpublishing.com

21  20  19  18          1  2  3  4

Ted Adams, CEO & Publisher
Greg Goldstein, President & COO
Robbie Robbins, EVP/Sr. Graphic Artist
Chris Ryall, Chief Creative Officer
David Hedgecock, Editor-in-Chief
Laurie Windrow, Senior Vice President of Sales & Marketing
Matthew Ruzicka, CPA, Chief Financial Officer
Lorelei Bunjes, VP of Digital Services
Jerry Bennington, VP of New Product Development

**IDW**
www.IDWPUBLISHING.com

**ACTIVISION**®

Facebook: **facebook.com/idwpublishing**
Twitter: **@idwpublishing**
YouTube: **youtube.com/idwpublishing**
Tumblr: **tumblr.idwpublishing.com**
Instagram: **instagram.com/idwpublishing**

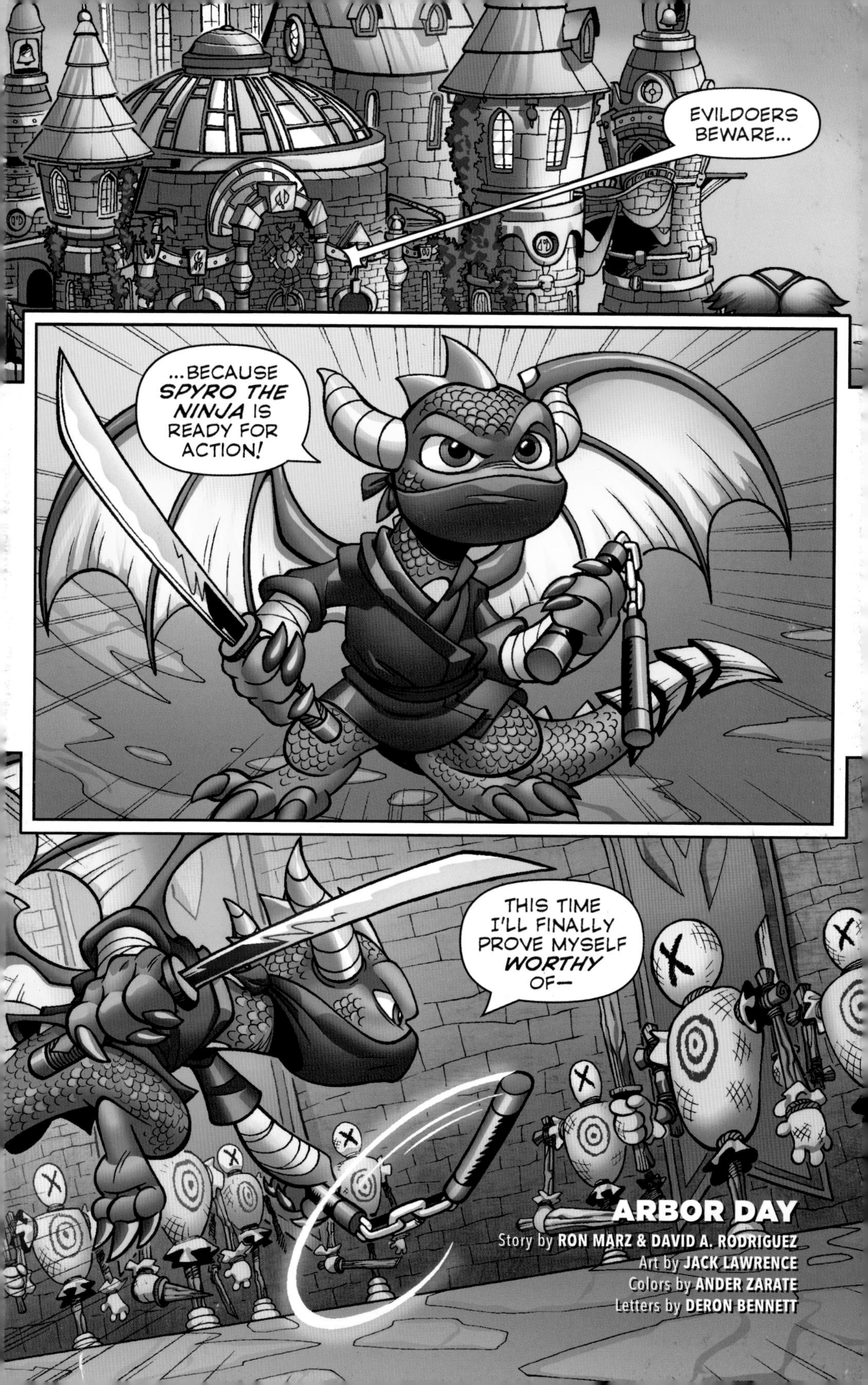
EVILDOERS BEWARE...
...BECAUSE SPYRO THE NINJA IS READY FOR ACTION!
THIS TIME I'LL FINALLY PROVE MYSELF WORTHY OF—
ARBOR DAY
Story by RON MARZ & DAVID A. RODRIGUEZ
Art by JACK LAWRENCE
Colors by ANDER ZARATE
Letters by DERON BENNETT

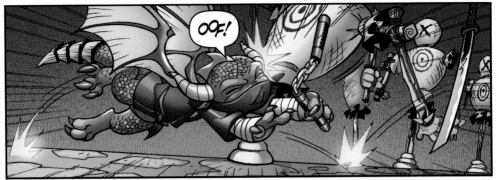

THAT... DID NOT GO AS *PLANNED*.

YOU CAN'T JUST *GIVE UP*, SPYRO.

I'M *NEVER* GOING TO MAKE A GOOD NINJA, STEALTH ELF, NO MATTER HOW MUCH YOU TRY TO TEACH ME.

I FEEL LIKE THE *ONLY* ONE AT SKYLANDER ACADEMY WHO'S NOT LEARNING ANYTHING.

SOME STUDENTS JUST NEED MORE *TIME*. IN YOUR CASE...

...A *LOT* MORE TIME.

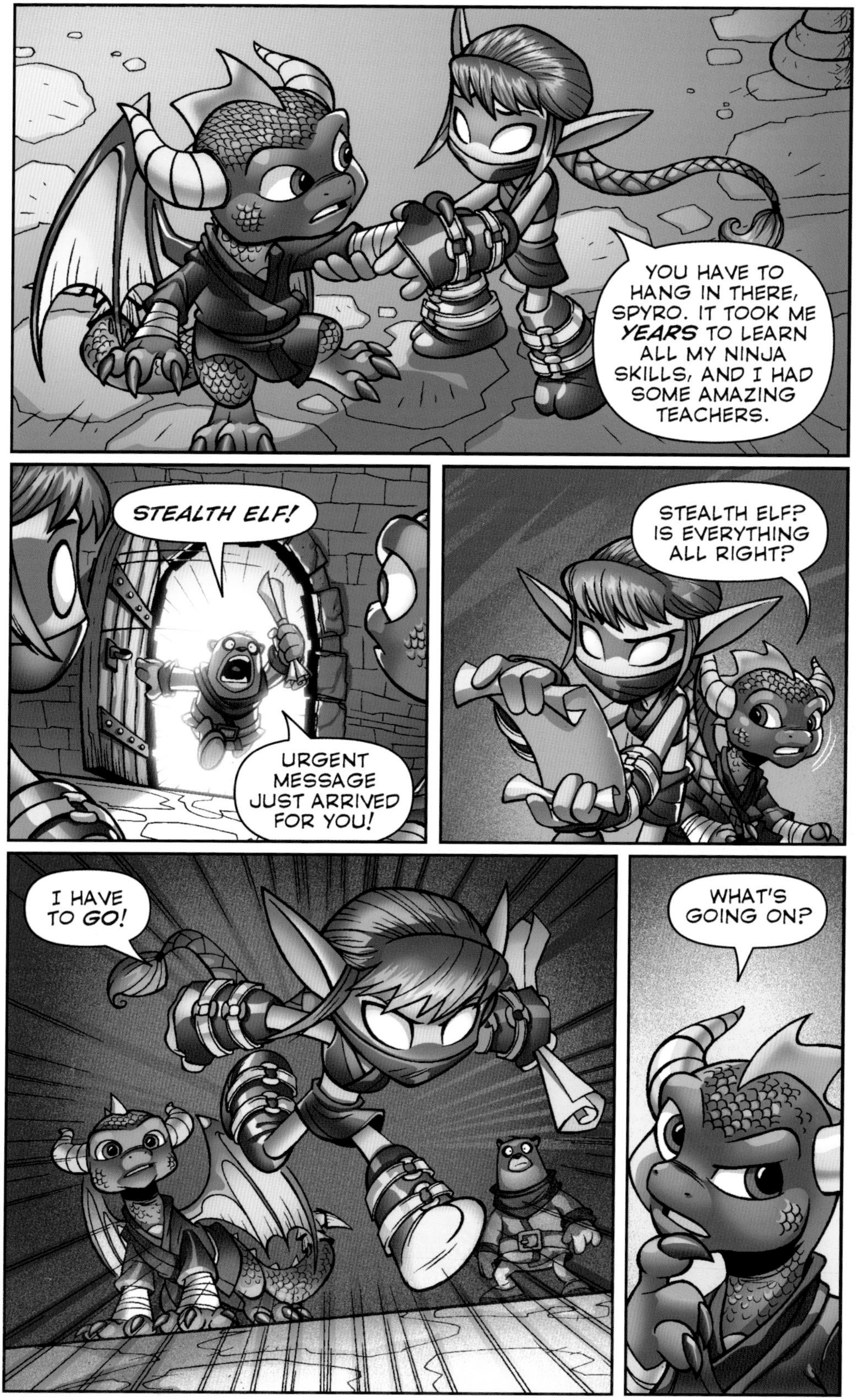
YOU HAVE TO HANG IN THERE, SPYRO. IT TOOK ME *YEARS* TO LEARN ALL MY NINJA SKILLS, AND I HAD SOME AMAZING TEACHERS.
*STEALTH ELF!*
URGENT MESSAGE JUST ARRIVED FOR YOU!
STEALTH ELF? IS EVERYTHING ALL RIGHT?
I HAVE TO *GO!*
WHAT'S GOING ON?

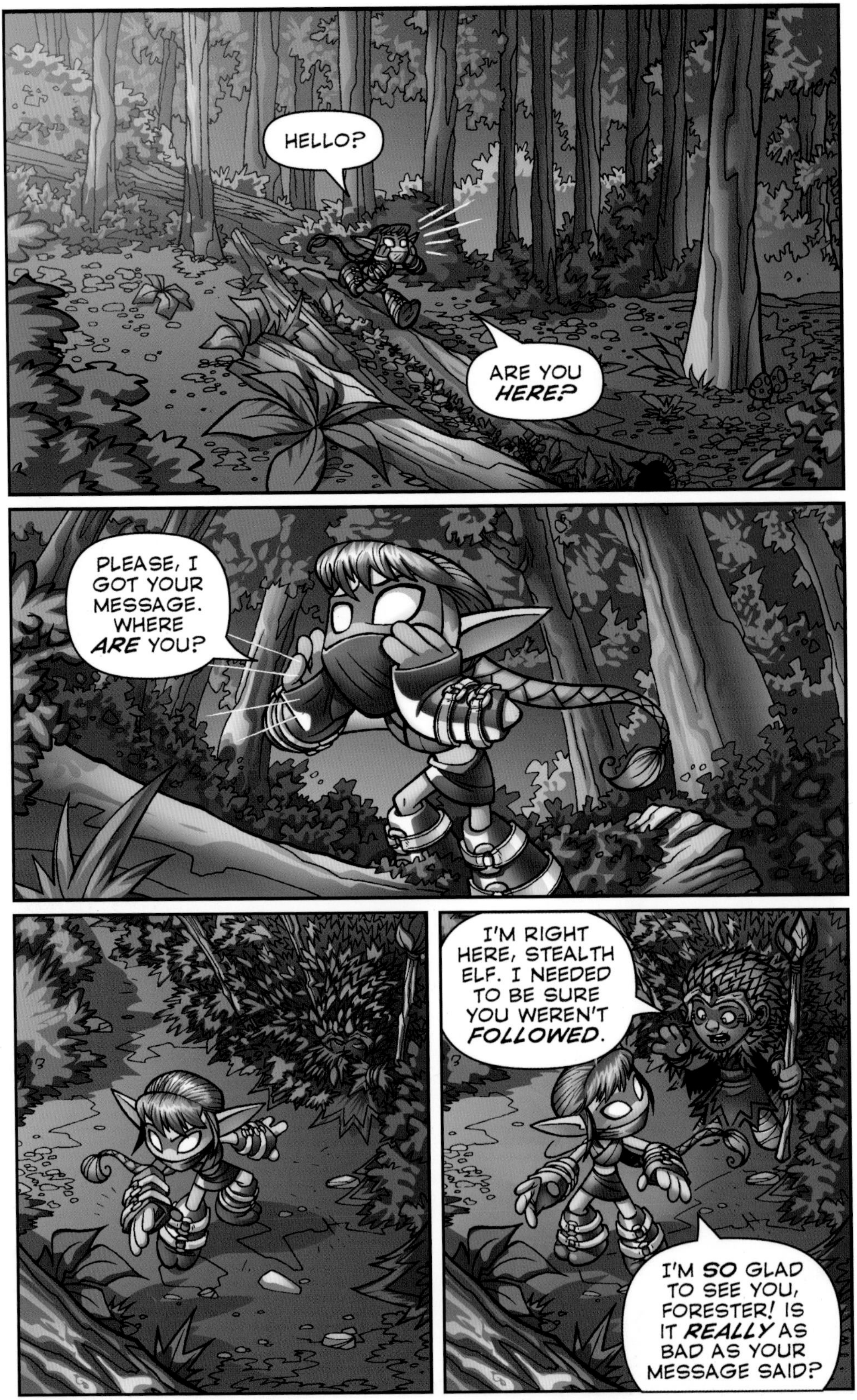
HELLO?
ARE YOU *HERE?*
PLEASE, I GOT YOUR MESSAGE. WHERE *ARE* YOU?
I'M RIGHT HERE, STEALTH ELF. I NEEDED TO BE SURE YOU WEREN'T *FOLLOWED*.
I'M **SO** GLAD TO SEE YOU, FORESTER! IS IT *REALLY* AS BAD AS YOUR MESSAGE SAID?

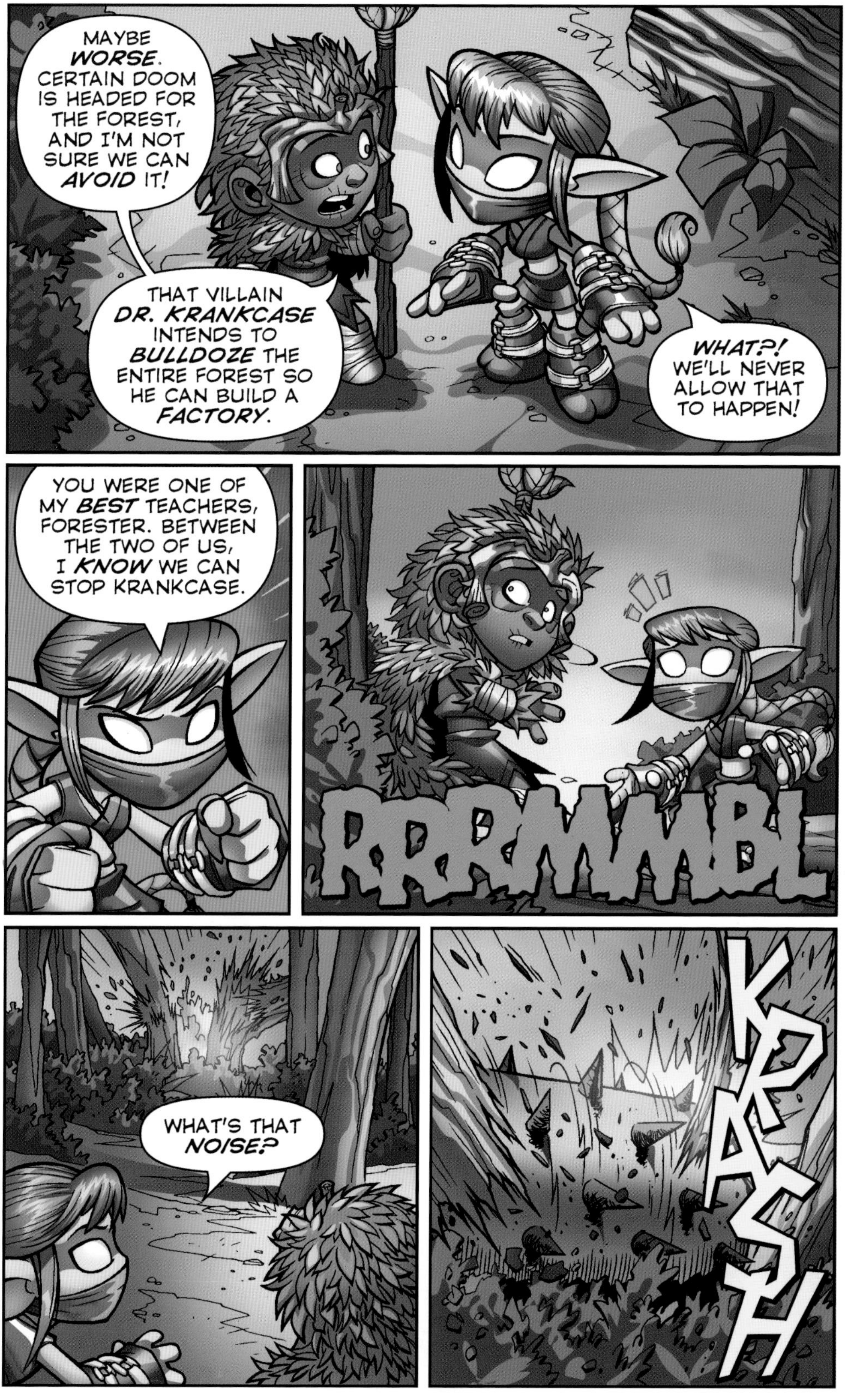
MAYBE WORSE. CERTAIN DOOM IS HEADED FOR THE FOREST, AND I'M NOT SURE WE CAN AVOID IT!
THAT VILLAIN DR. KRANKCASE INTENDS TO BULLDOZE THE ENTIRE FOREST SO HE CAN BUILD A FACTORY.
WHAT?! WE'LL NEVER ALLOW THAT TO HAPPEN!
YOU WERE ONE OF MY BEST TEACHERS, FORESTER. BETWEEN THE TWO OF US, I KNOW WE CAN STOP KRANKCASE.
RRRMMBL
WHAT'S THAT NOISE?
KRASH

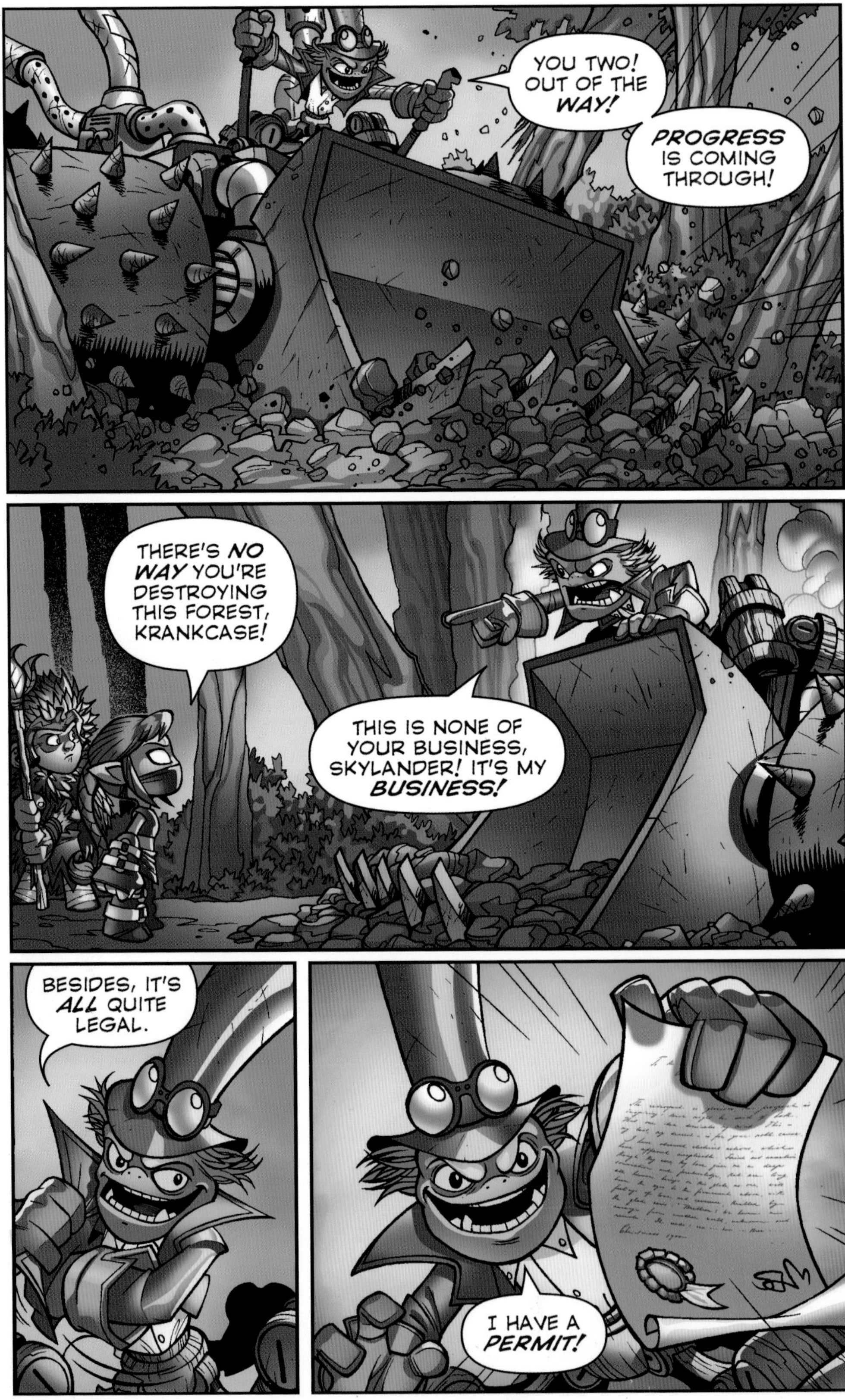
YOU TWO! OUT OF THE WAY!
PROGRESS IS COMING THROUGH!
THERE'S NO WAY YOU'RE DESTROYING THIS FOREST, KRANKCASE!
THIS IS NONE OF YOUR BUSINESS, SKYLANDER! IT'S MY BUSINESS!
BESIDES, IT'S ALL QUITE LEGAL.
I HAVE A PERMIT!

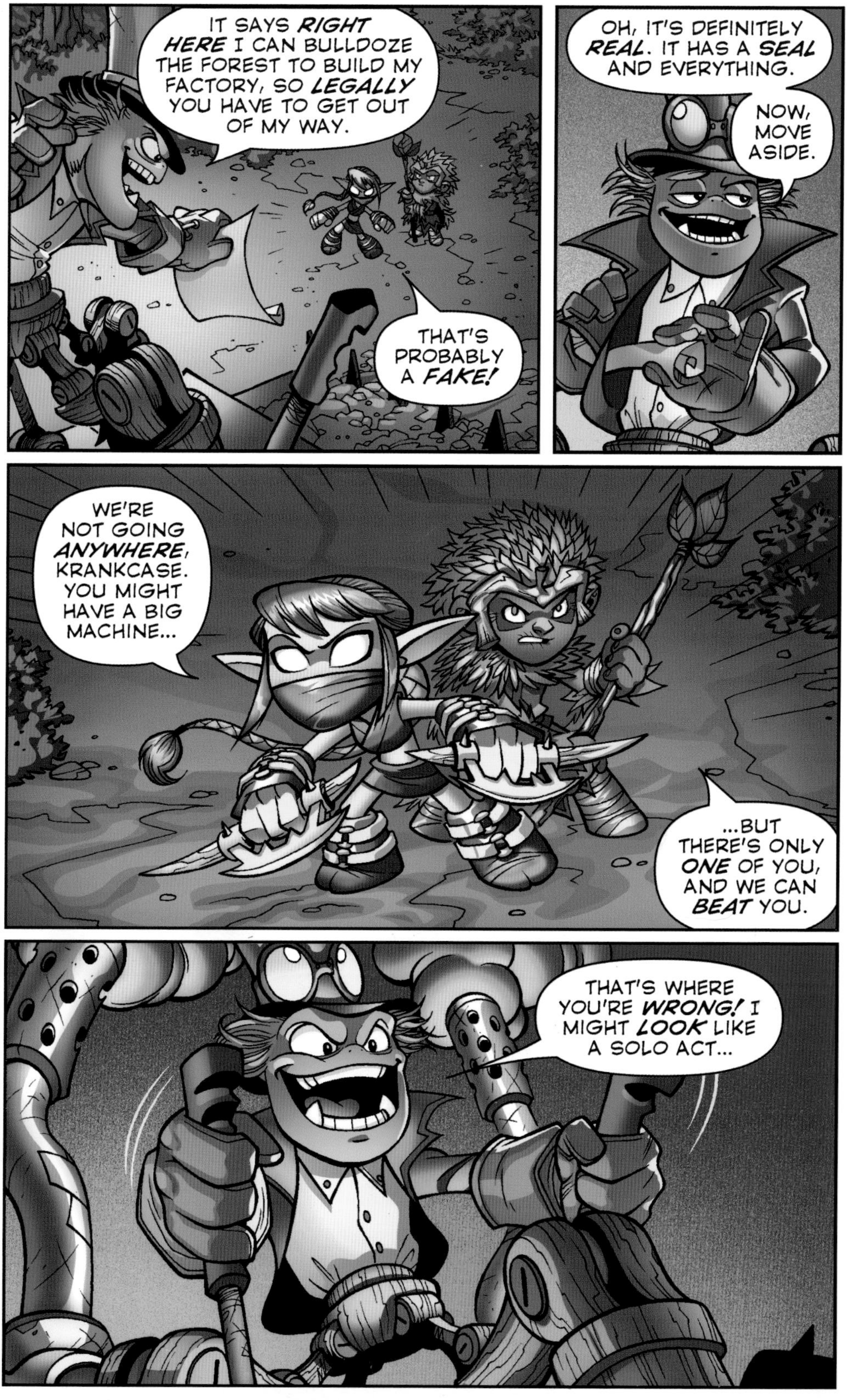

IT SAYS *RIGHT HERE* I CAN BULLDOZE THE FOREST TO BUILD MY FACTORY, SO *LEGALLY* YOU HAVE TO GET OUT OF MY WAY.
THAT'S PROBABLY A *FAKE!*
OH, IT'S DEFINITELY *REAL*. IT HAS A *SEAL* AND EVERYTHING.
NOW, MOVE ASIDE.
WE'RE NOT GOING *ANYWHERE*, KRANKCASE. YOU MIGHT HAVE A BIG MACHINE...
...BUT THERE'S ONLY *ONE* OF YOU, AND WE CAN *BEAT* YOU.
THAT'S WHERE YOU'RE *WRONG!* I MIGHT *LOOK* LIKE A SOLO ACT...

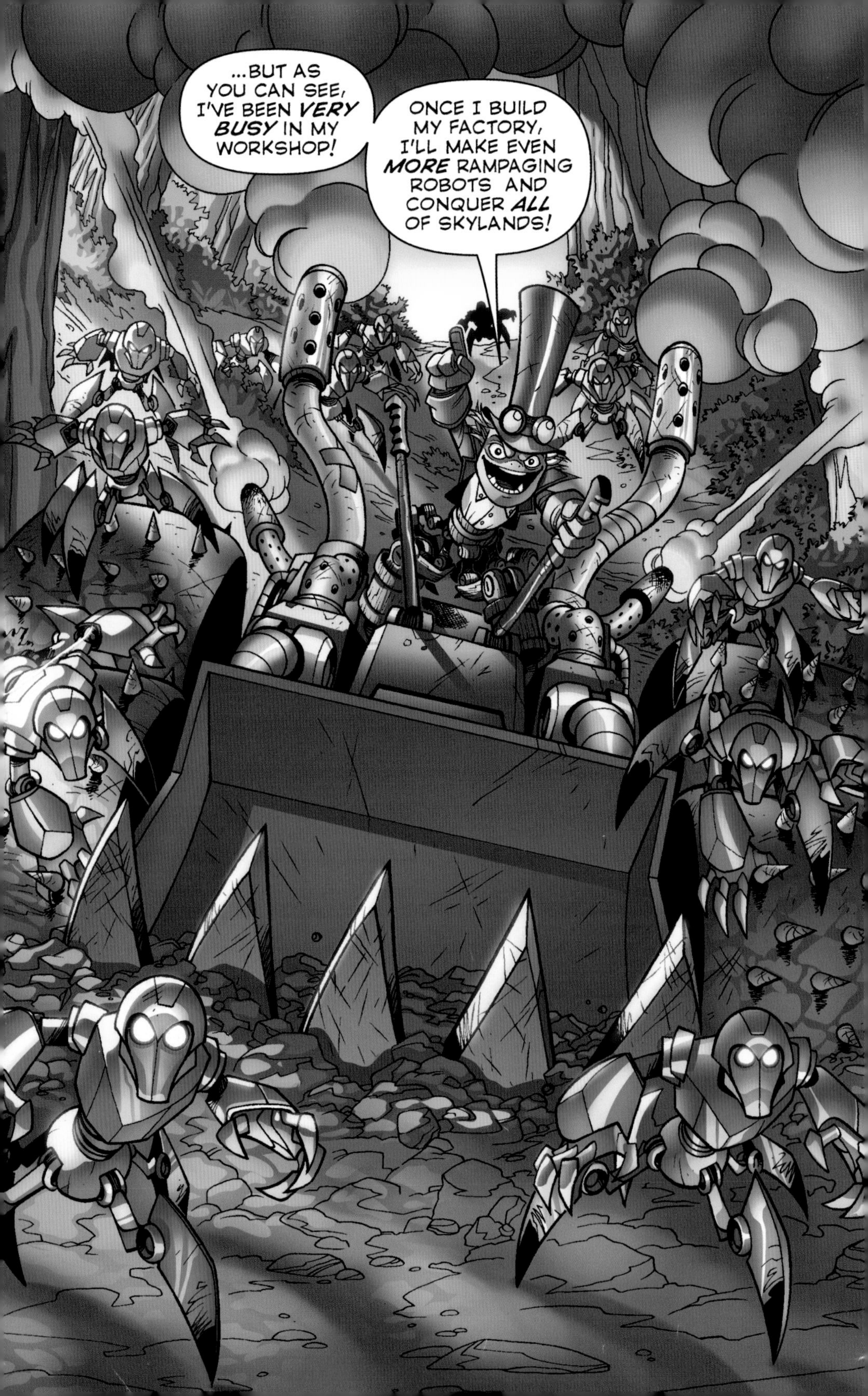
...BUT AS YOU CAN SEE, I'VE BEEN *VERY* *BUSY* IN MY WORKSHOP!
ONCE I BUILD MY FACTORY, I'LL MAKE EVEN *MORE* RAMPAGING ROBOTS AND CONQUER *ALL* OF SKYLANDS!

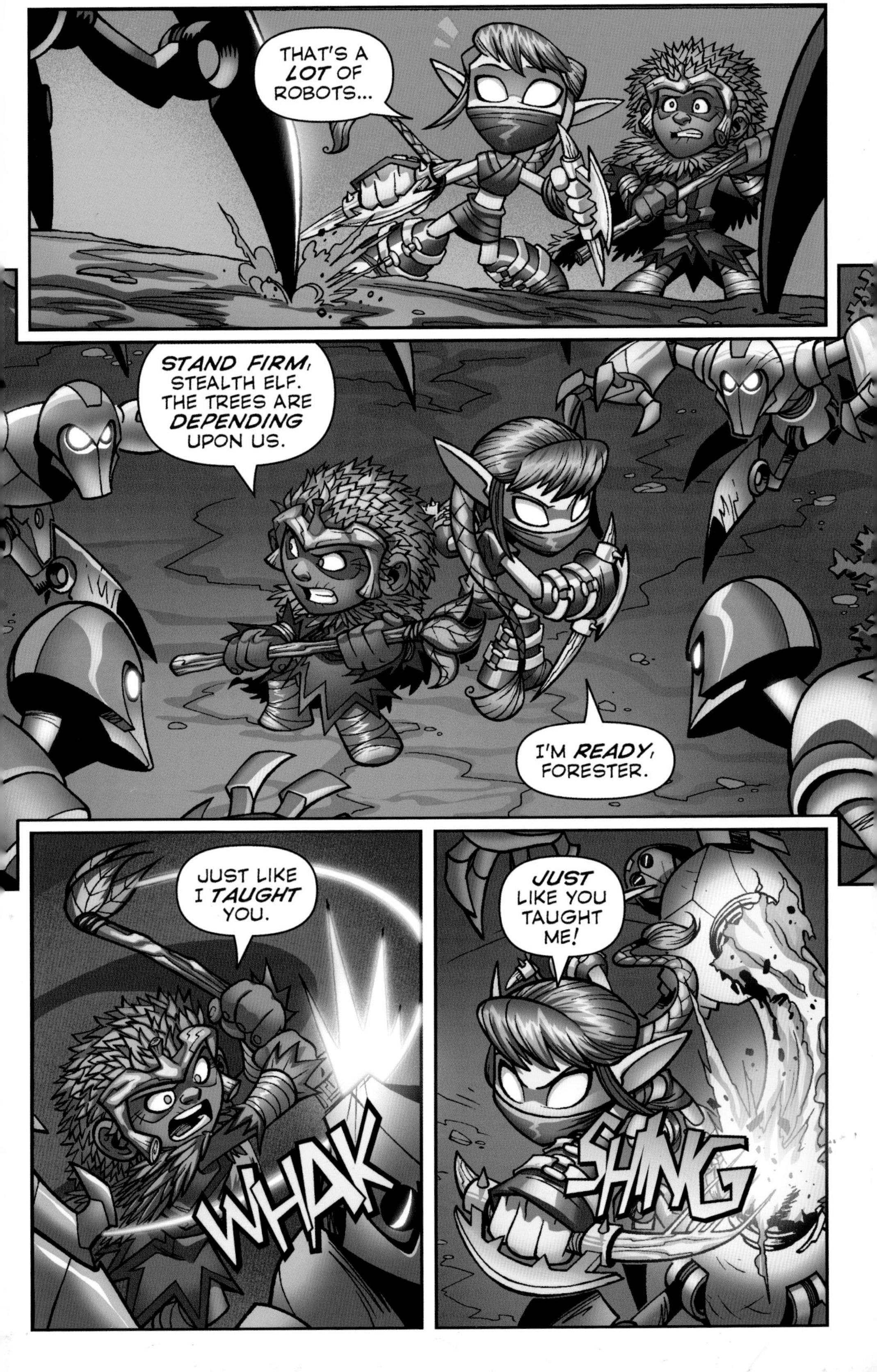
THAT'S A *LOT* OF ROBOTS...
*STAND FIRM*, STEALTH ELF. THE TREES ARE *DEPENDING* UPON US.
I'M *READY*, FORESTER.
JUST LIKE I *TAUGHT* YOU.
WHAK
*JUST* LIKE YOU TAUGHT ME!
SHING

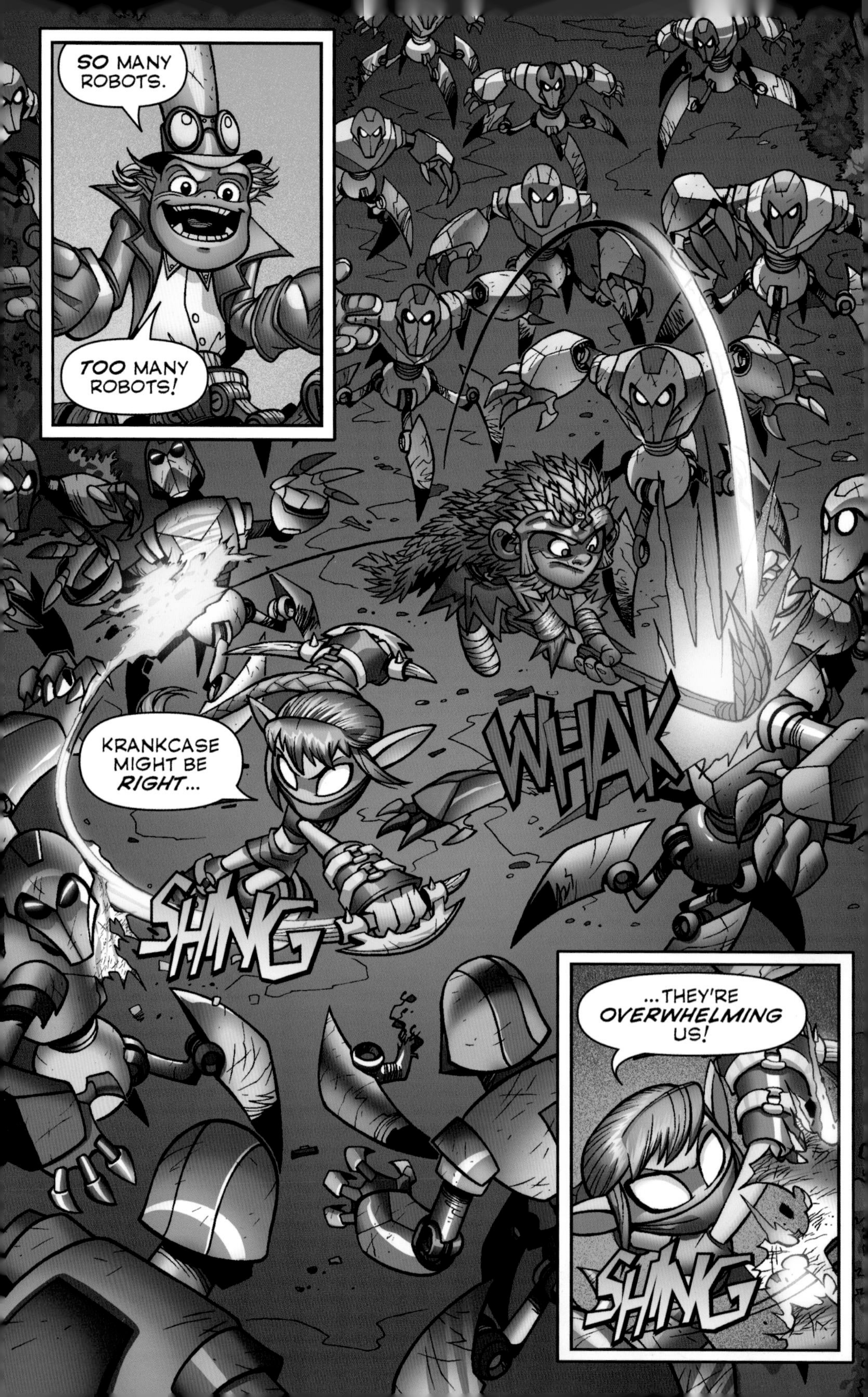
SO MANY ROBOTS.
TOO MANY ROBOTS!
KRANKCASE MIGHT BE RIGHT...
WHAK
SHING
...THEY'RE OVERWHELMING US!
SHING

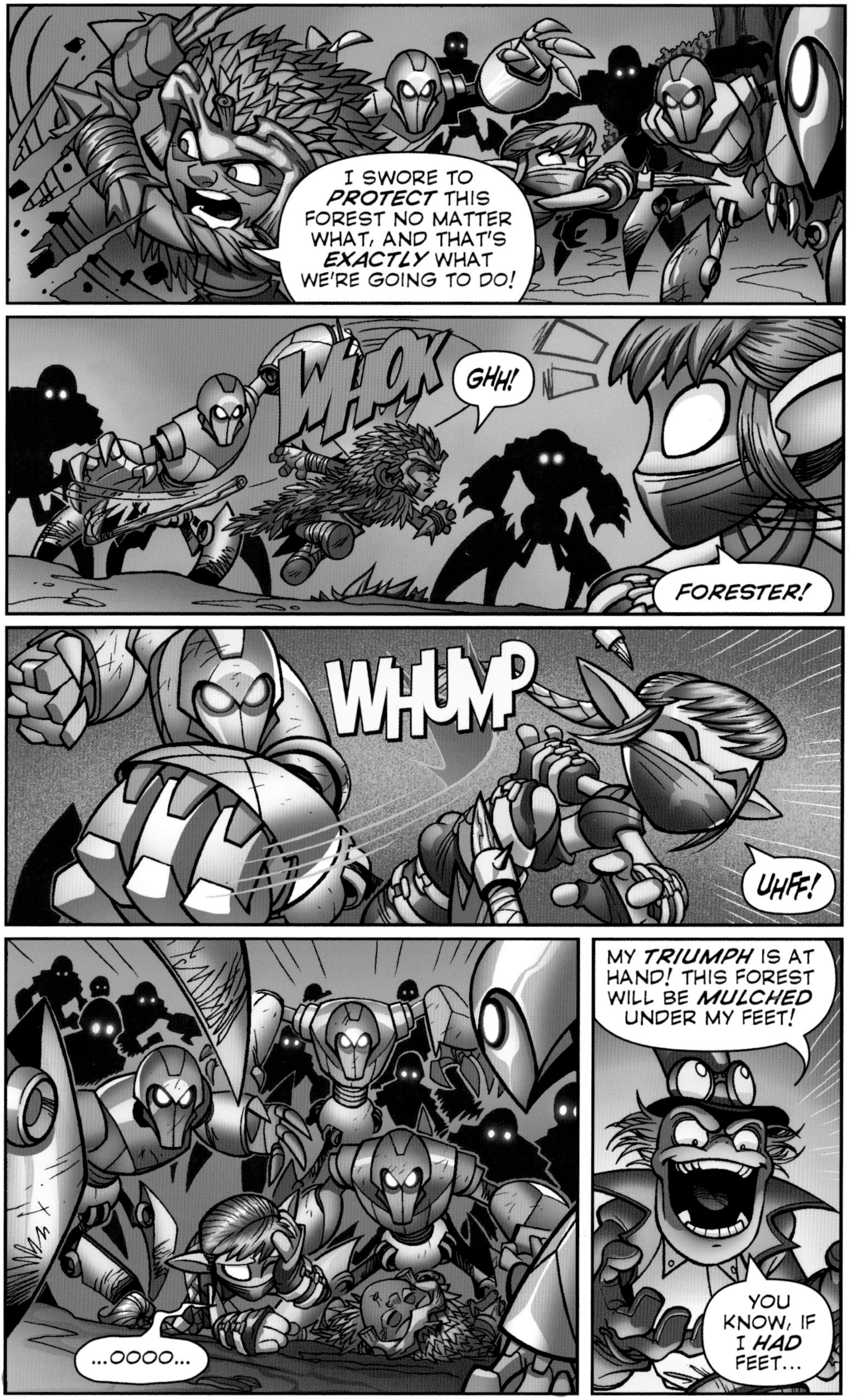
I SWORE TO PROTECT THIS FOREST NO MATTER WHAT, AND THAT'S EXACTLY WHAT WE'RE GOING TO DO!
WHOK
GHH!
FORESTER!
WHUMP
UHFF!
...OOOO...
MY TRIUMPH IS AT HAND! THIS FOREST WILL BE MULCHED UNDER MY FEET!
YOU KNOW, IF I HAD FEET...

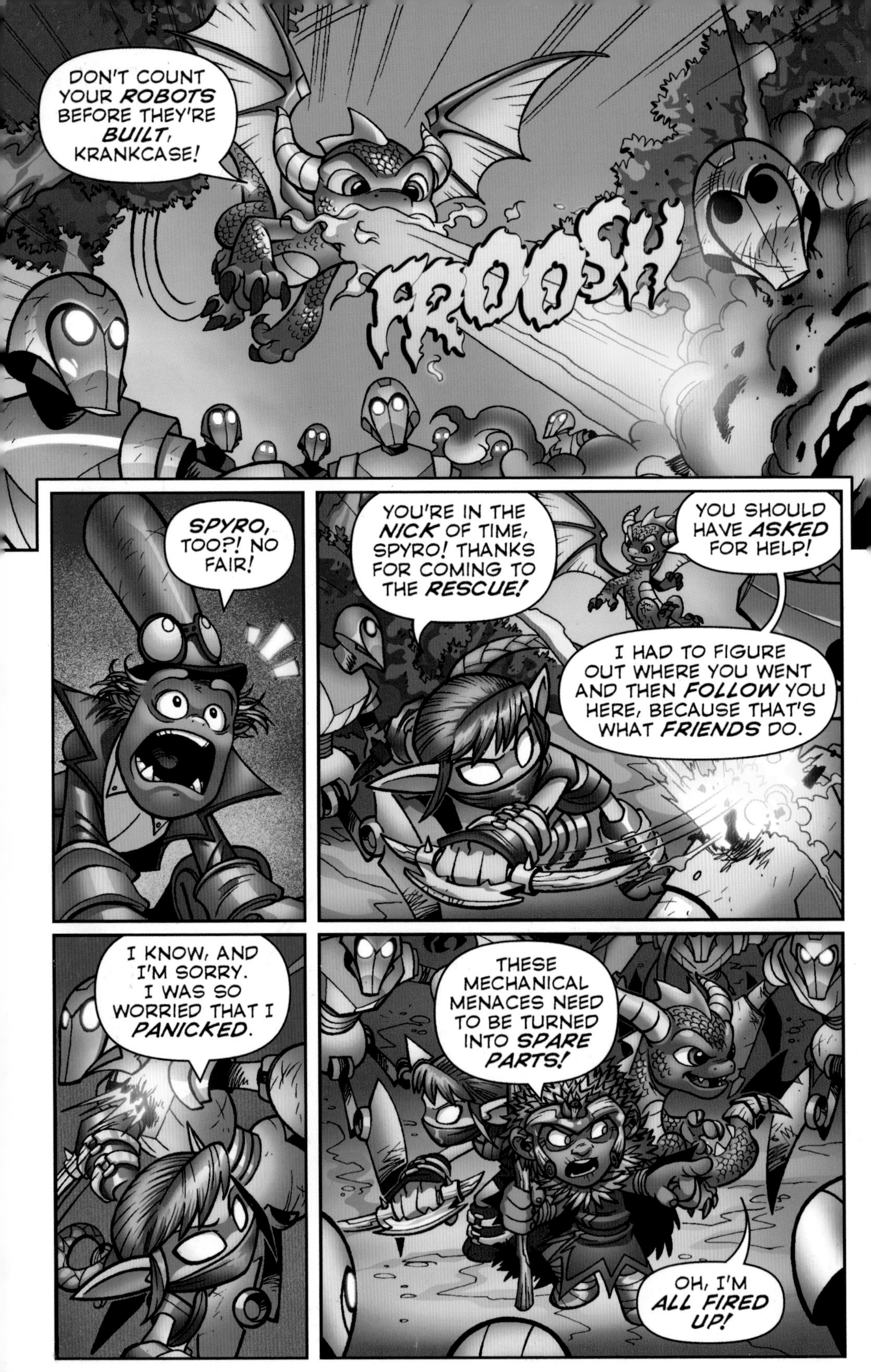
DON'T COUNT YOUR ROBOTS BEFORE THEY'RE BUILT, KRANKCASE!
FROOSH
SPYRO, TOO?! NO FAIR!
YOU'RE IN THE NICK OF TIME, SPYRO! THANKS FOR COMING TO THE RESCUE!
YOU SHOULD HAVE ASKED FOR HELP!
I HAD TO FIGURE OUT WHERE YOU WENT AND THEN FOLLOW YOU HERE, BECAUSE THAT'S WHAT FRIENDS DO.
I KNOW, AND I'M SORRY. I WAS SO WORRIED THAT I PANICKED.
THESE MECHANICAL MENACES NEED TO BE TURNED INTO SPARE PARTS!
OH, I'M ALL FIRED UP!

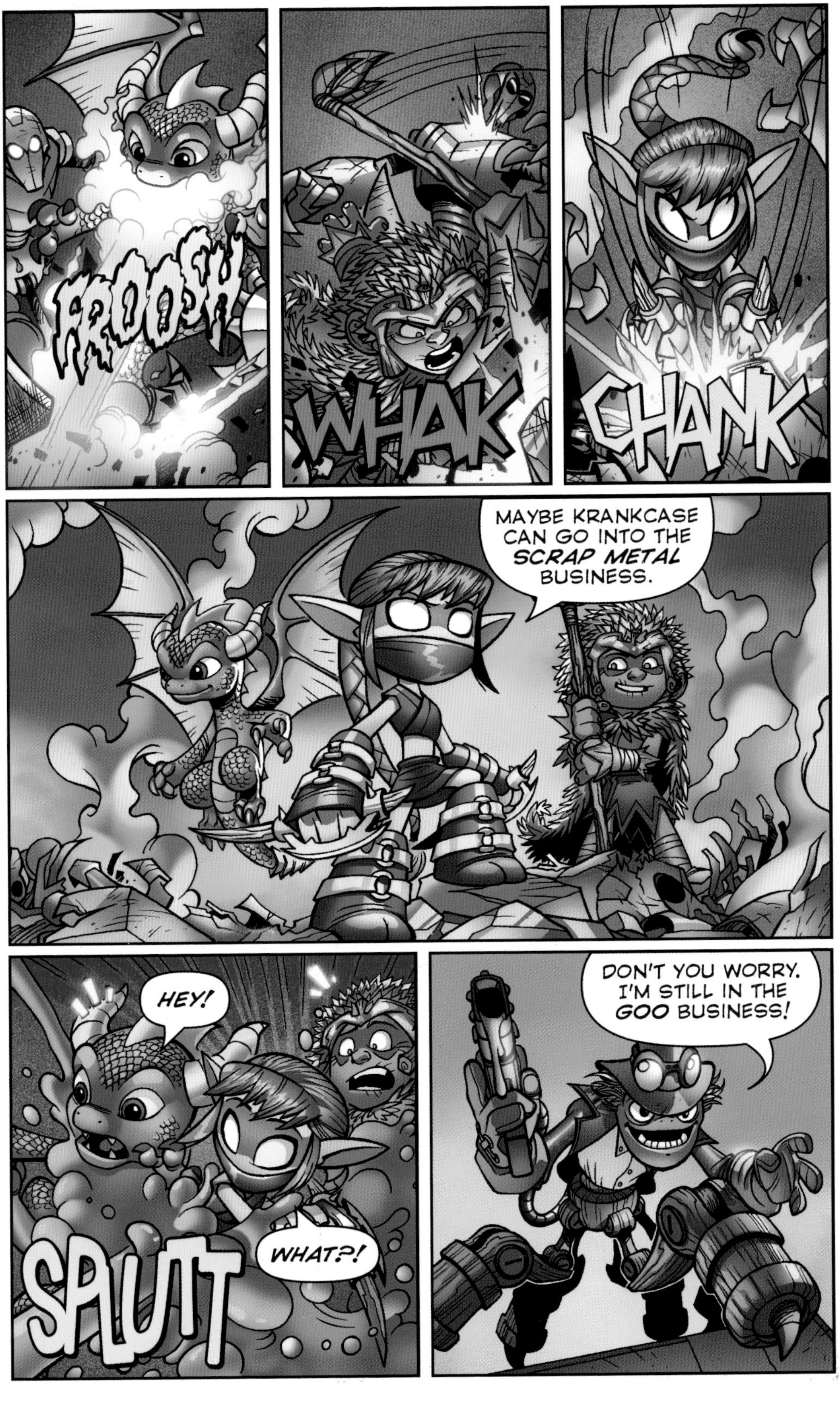
FROOSH
WHAK
CHANK
MAYBE KRANKCASE CAN GO INTO THE *SCRAP METAL* BUSINESS.
SPLUTT
*HEY!*
*WHAT?!*
DON'T YOU WORRY. I'M STILL IN THE *GOO* BUSINESS!

WHILE MY PATENTED *GOOEY GLOP* HOLDS YOU PESTS IN PLACE...

...MY CRUSHER CAN FINALLY GET CRANKED UP! SO LONG, SKYLANDERS!

I CAN'T *BUDGE!*

I WOULDN'T BE MUCH OF A *NINJA*...

...IF I COULDN'T GET *GONE* FROM SOME GOO!

I'LL SAY *THIS* FOR YOU, STEALTH ELF, YOU DON'T GIVE UP...

SPLUTT

...EVEN WHEN YOU'VE ALREADY *LOST!*

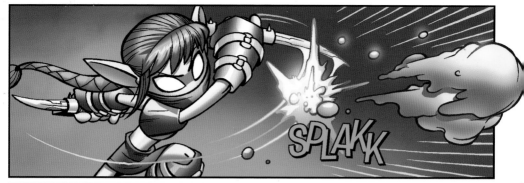

**SPLAKK**

ARRGH!

**SPLATT**

YOUR CRUSHER HAS CRUSHED ITS *LAST* TREE, KRANKCASE!

NOW LET'S SEE THIS *"PERMIT"* OF YOURS.

THINK I'M STARTING TO WRIGGLE MY *TAIL* FREE...

JUST AS I THOUGHT...

...*FAKE*.

CAN'T BLAME A GUY FOR *TRYING*.

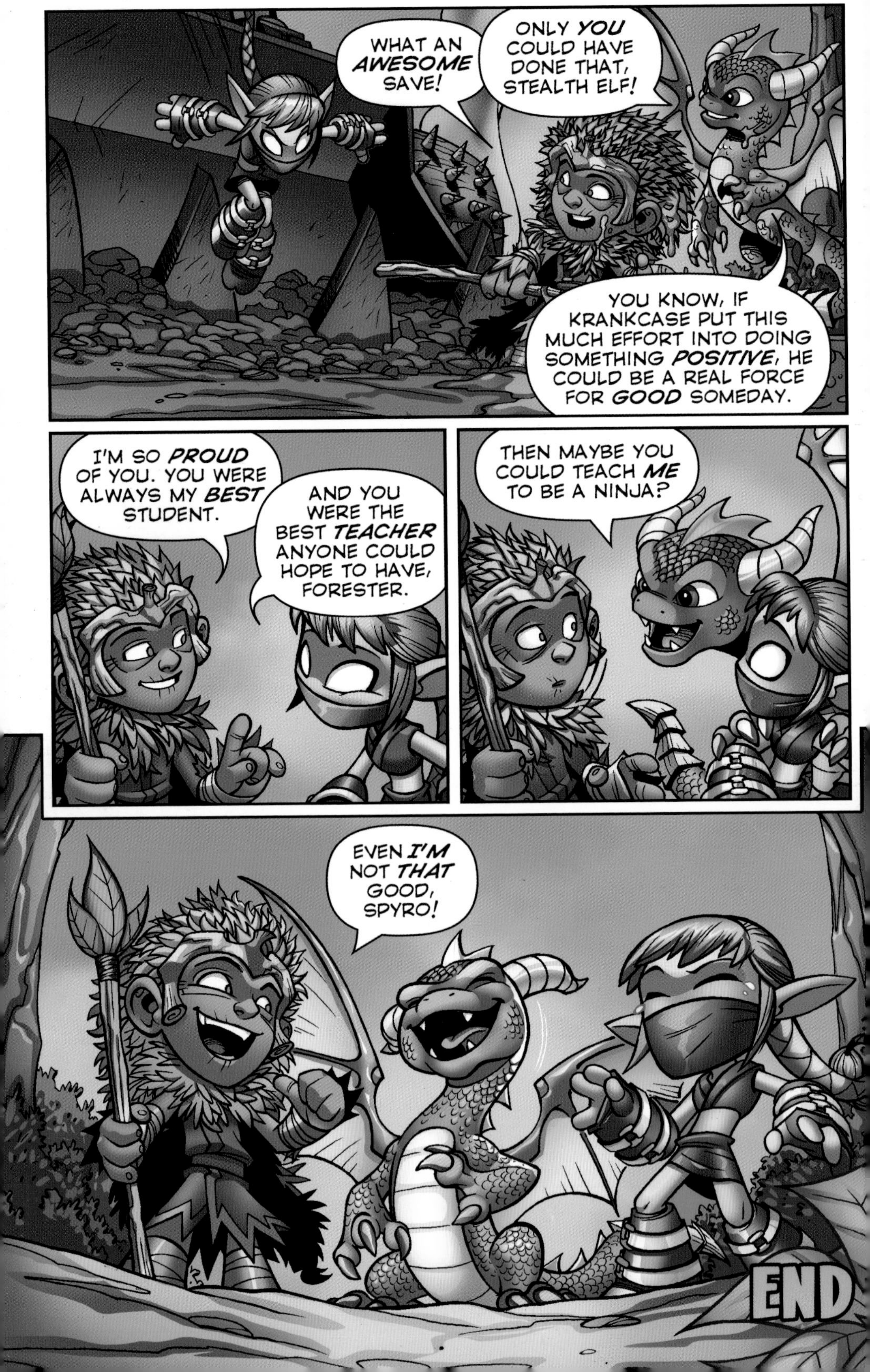
WHAT AN AWESOME SAVE!
ONLY YOU COULD HAVE DONE THAT, STEALTH ELF!
YOU KNOW, IF KRANKCASE PUT THIS MUCH EFFORT INTO DOING SOMETHING POSITIVE, HE COULD BE A REAL FORCE FOR GOOD SOMEDAY.
I'M SO PROUD OF YOU. YOU WERE ALWAYS MY BEST STUDENT.
AND YOU WERE THE BEST TEACHER ANYONE COULD HOPE TO HAVE, FORESTER.
THEN MAYBE YOU COULD TEACH ME TO BE A NINJA?
EVEN I'M NOT THAT GOOD, SPYRO!
END

# FULL BLAST

Story by RON MARZ & DAVID A. RODRIGUEZ
Art by SALVATORE COSTANZA
Colors by JORDI ESCUIN
Letters by DERON BENNETT

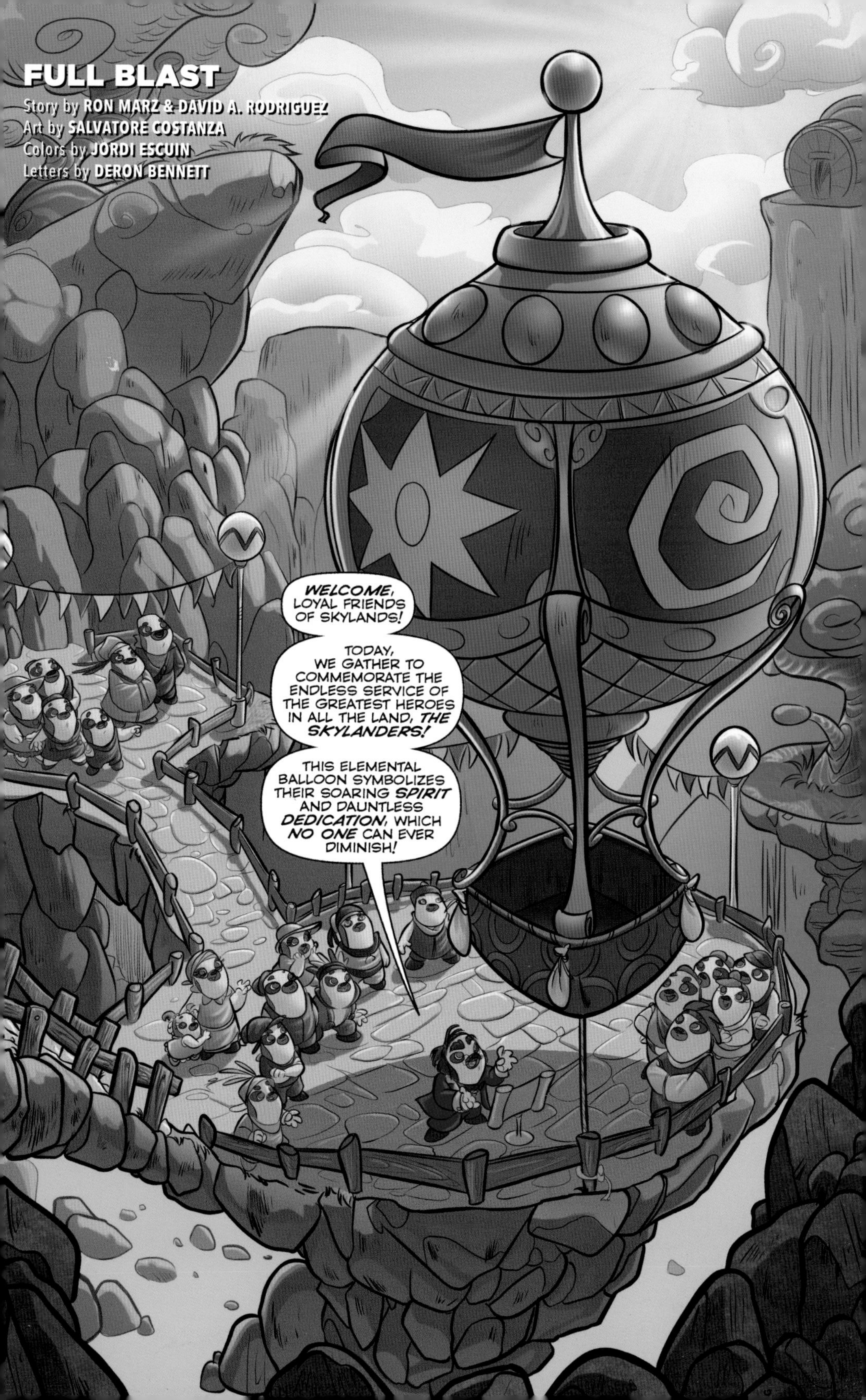
WELCOME, LOYAL FRIENDS OF SKYLANDS!
TODAY, WE GATHER TO COMMEMORATE THE ENDLESS SERVICE OF THE GREATEST HEROES IN ALL THE LAND, THE SKYLANDERS!
THIS ELEMENTAL BALLOON SYMBOLIZES THEIR SOARING SPIRIT AND DAUNTLESS DEDICATION, WHICH NO ONE CAN EVER DIMINISH!

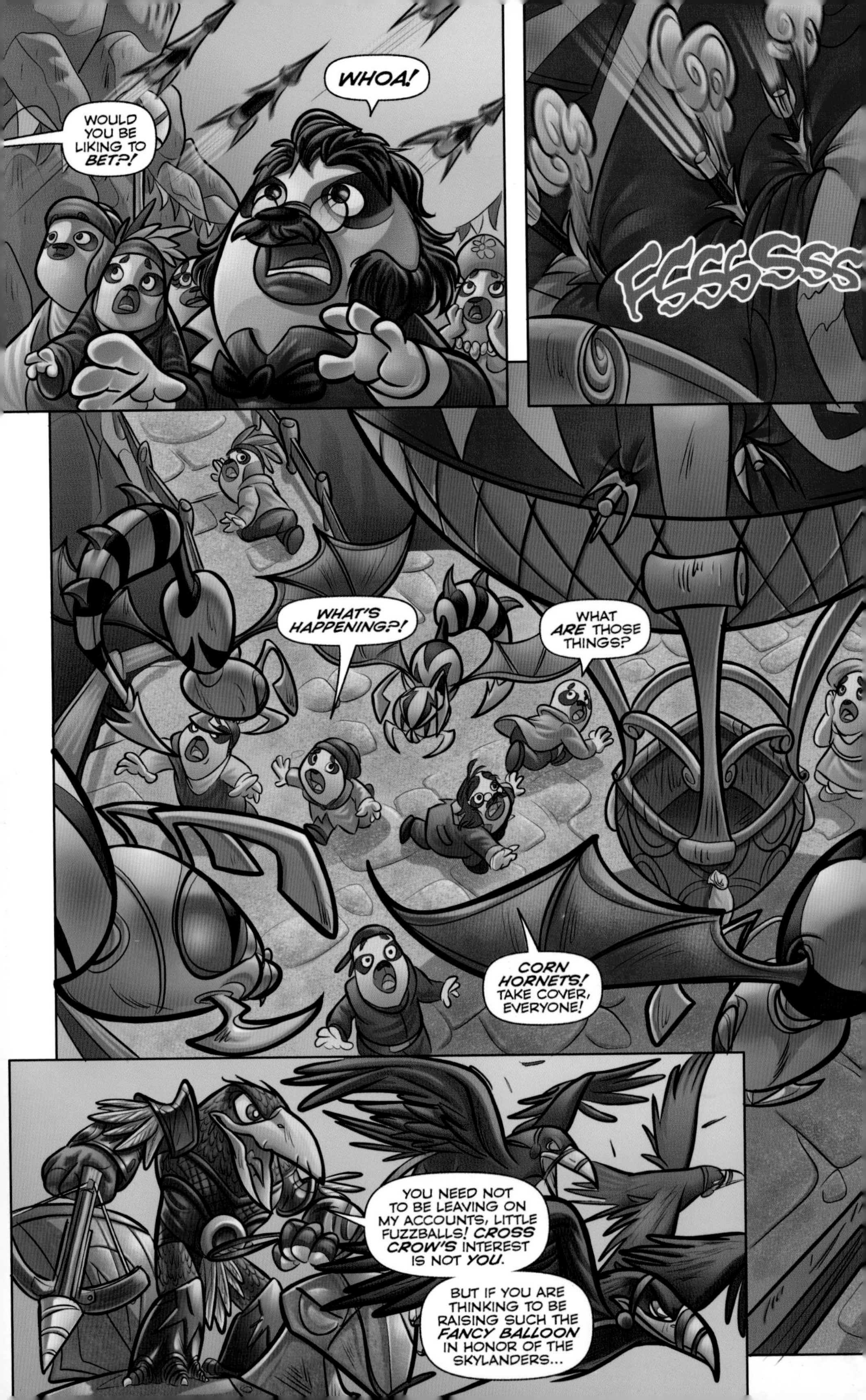
WOULD YOU BE LIKING TO BET?!
WHOA!
FSSSSSS
WHAT'S HAPPENING?!
WHAT ARE THOSE THINGS?
CORN HORNETS! TAKE COVER, EVERYONE!
YOU NEED NOT TO BE LEAVING ON MY ACCOUNTS, LITTLE FUZZBALLS! CROSS CROW'S INTEREST IS NOT YOU.
BUT IF YOU ARE THINKING TO BE RAISING SUCH THE FANCY BALLOON IN HONOR OF THE SKYLANDERS...

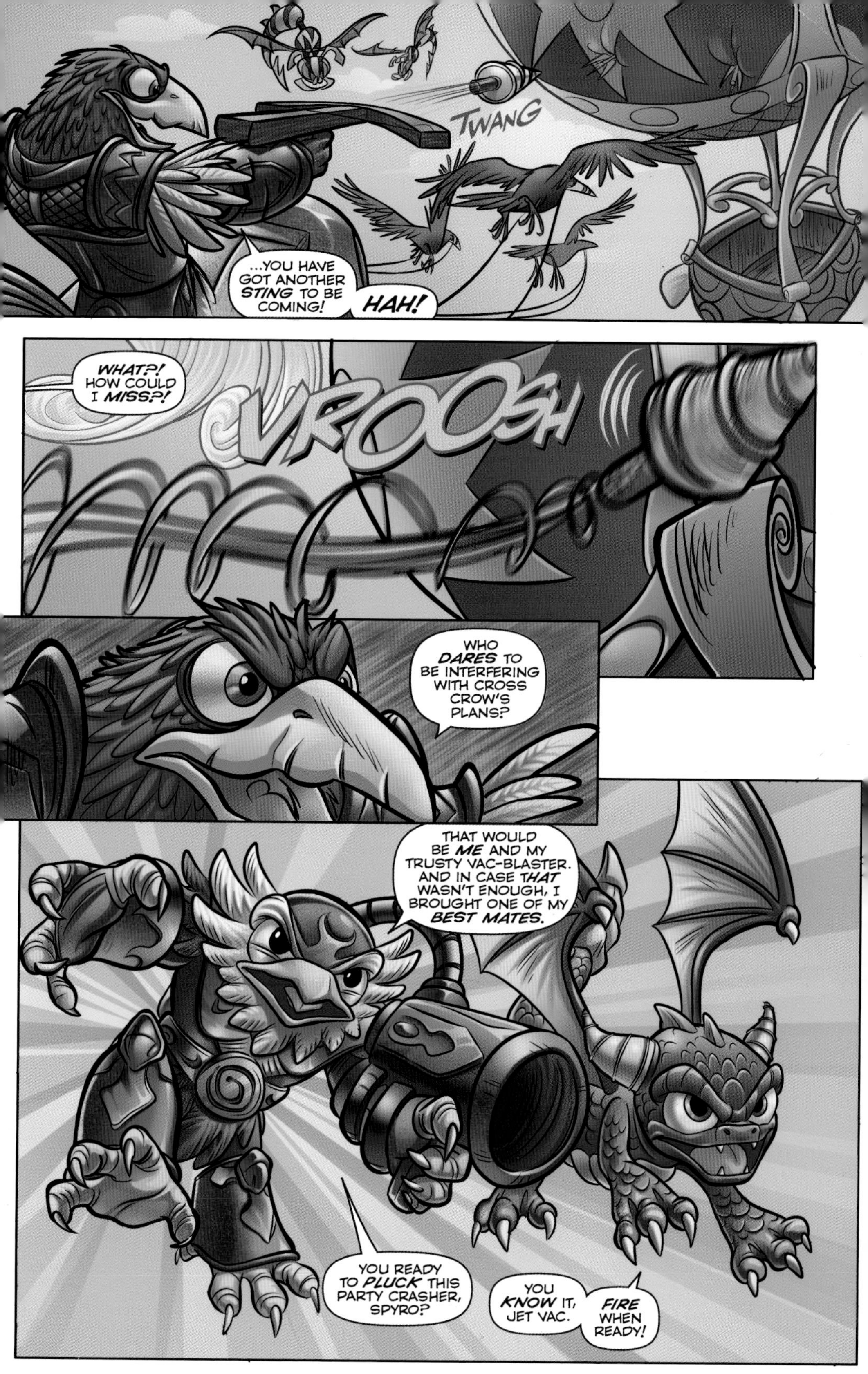
TWANG
...YOU HAVE GOT ANOTHER STING TO BE COMING!
HAH!
WHAT?! HOW COULD I MISS?!
VROOSH
WHO DARES TO BE INTERFERING WITH CROSS CROW'S PLANS?
THAT WOULD BE ME AND MY TRUSTY VAC-BLASTER. AND IN CASE THAT WASN'T ENOUGH, I BROUGHT ONE OF MY BEST MATES.
YOU READY TO PLUCK THIS PARTY CRASHER, SPYRO?
YOU KNOW IT, JET VAC.
FIRE WHEN READY!

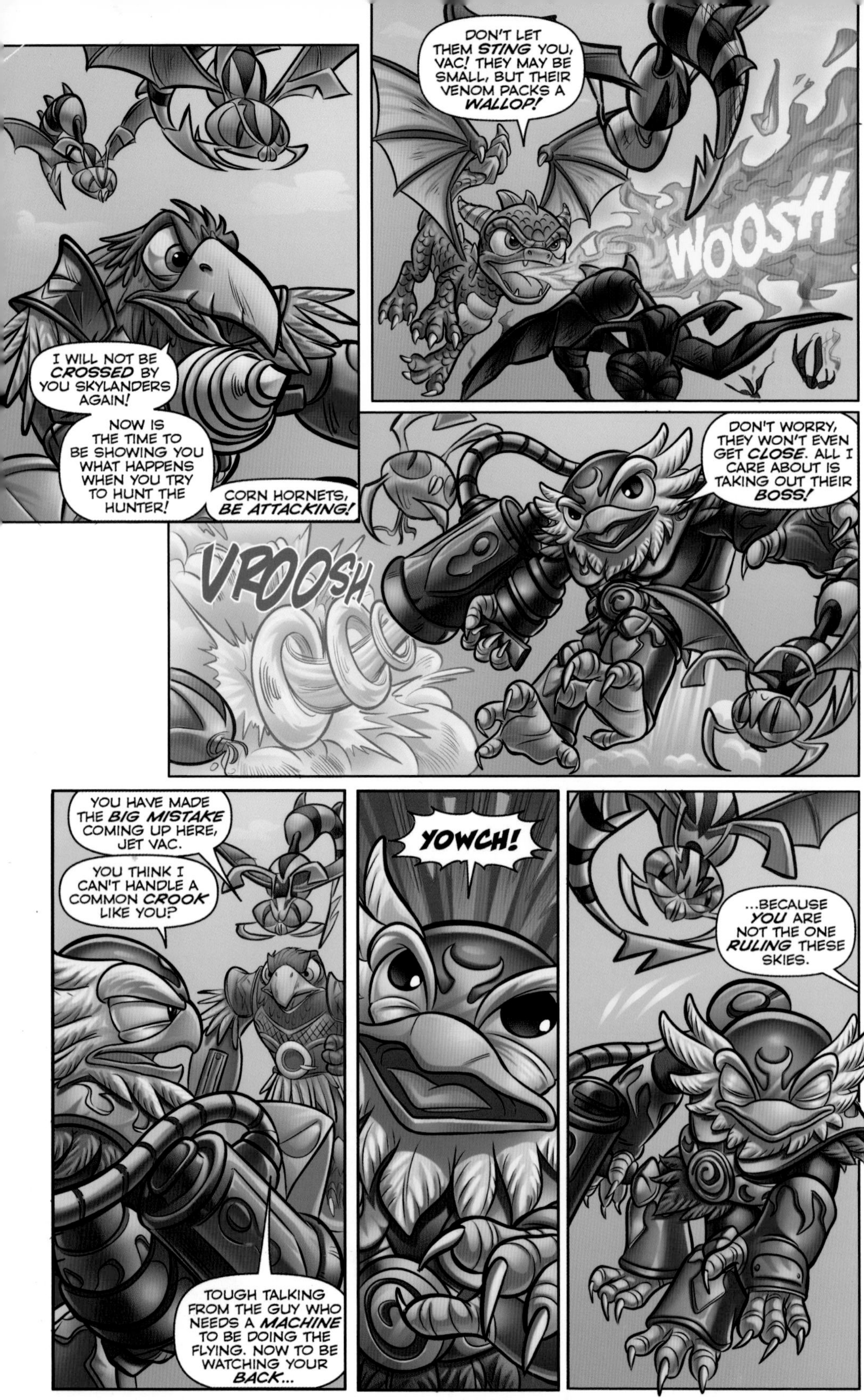
I WILL NOT BE CROSSED BY YOU SKYLANDERS AGAIN!
NOW IS THE TIME TO BE SHOWING YOU WHAT HAPPENS WHEN YOU TRY TO HUNT THE HUNTER!
CORN HORNETS, BE ATTACKING!
DON'T LET THEM STING YOU, VAC! THEY MAY BE SMALL, BUT THEIR VENOM PACKS A WALLOP!
WOOSH
DON'T WORRY, THEY WON'T EVEN GET CLOSE. ALL I CARE ABOUT IS TAKING OUT THEIR BOSS!
VROOSH
YOU HAVE MADE THE BIG MISTAKE COMING UP HERE, JET VAC.
YOU THINK I CAN'T HANDLE A COMMON CROOK LIKE YOU?
TOUGH TALKING FROM THE GUY WHO NEEDS A MACHINE TO BE DOING THE FLYING. NOW TO BE WATCHING YOUR BACK...
YOWCH!
...BECAUSE YOU ARE NOT THE ONE RULING THESE SKIES.

YOU NEED NOT TO BE WORRYING, THE CORN HORNET VENOM WILL KEEP YOU *KNOCKED OUT...*

...ALL THE WAY TO THE *GROUND!*

JET VAC!

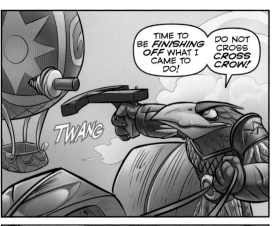

TIME TO BE *FINISHING OFF* WHAT I CAME TO DO!

DO NOT CROSS *CROSS CROW!*

*TWANG*

HANG ON, PAL! I'M *COMING!*

*FSSSSSS*

FALLING SO FAST...

...CAN'T QUITE *REACH...*

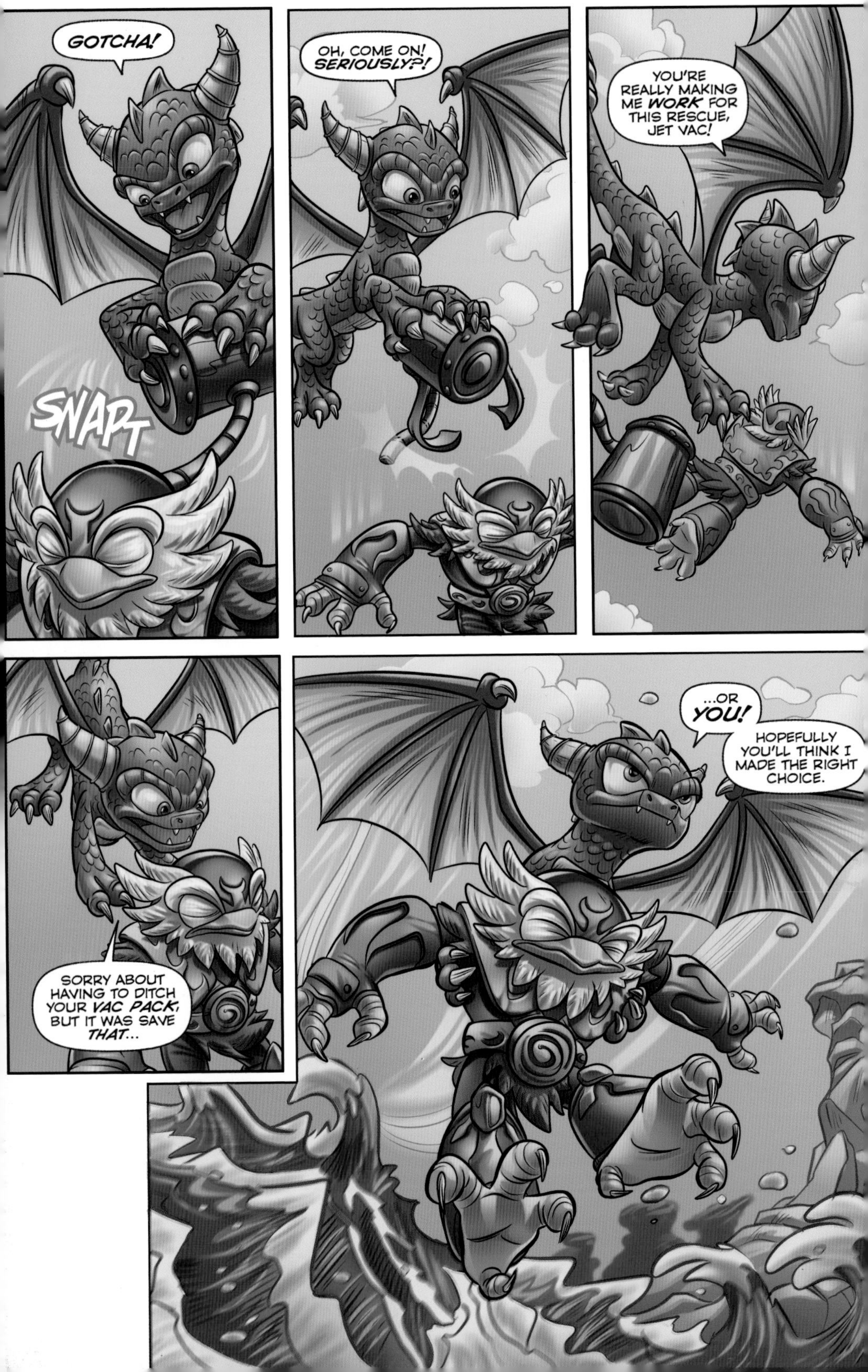
GOTCHA!
SNAPT
OH, COME ON! SERIOUSLY?!
YOU'RE REALLY MAKING ME WORK FOR THIS RESCUE, JET VAC!
SORRY ABOUT HAVING TO DITCH YOUR VAC PACK, BUT IT WAS SAVE THAT...
...OR YOU!
HOPEFULLY YOU'LL THINK I MADE THE RIGHT CHOICE.

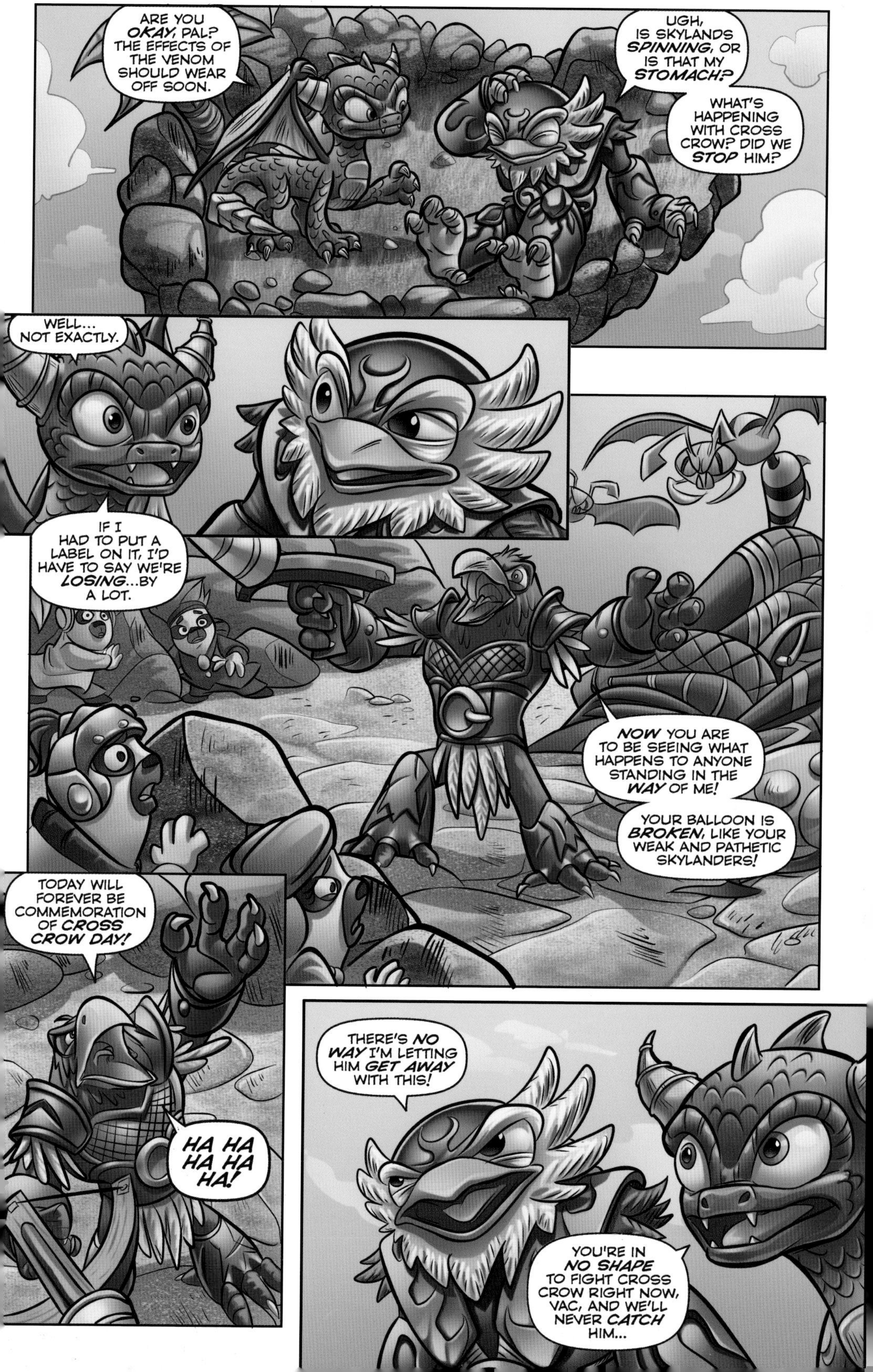
ARE YOU OKAY, PAL? THE EFFECTS OF THE VENOM SHOULD WEAR OFF SOON.
UGH, IS SKYLANDS SPINNING, OR IS THAT MY STOMACH?
WHAT'S HAPPENING WITH CROSS CROW? DID WE STOP HIM?
WELL... NOT EXACTLY.
IF I HAD TO PUT A LABEL ON IT, I'D HAVE TO SAY WE'RE LOSING...BY A LOT.
NOW YOU ARE TO BE SEEING WHAT HAPPENS TO ANYONE STANDING IN THE WAY OF ME!
YOUR BALLOON IS BROKEN, LIKE YOUR WEAK AND PATHETIC SKYLANDERS!
TODAY WILL FOREVER BE COMMEMORATION OF CROSS CROW DAY!
HA HA HA HA HA!
THERE'S NO WAY I'M LETTING HIM GET AWAY WITH THIS!
YOU'RE IN NO SHAPE TO FIGHT CROSS CROW RIGHT NOW, VAC, AND WE'LL NEVER CATCH HIM...

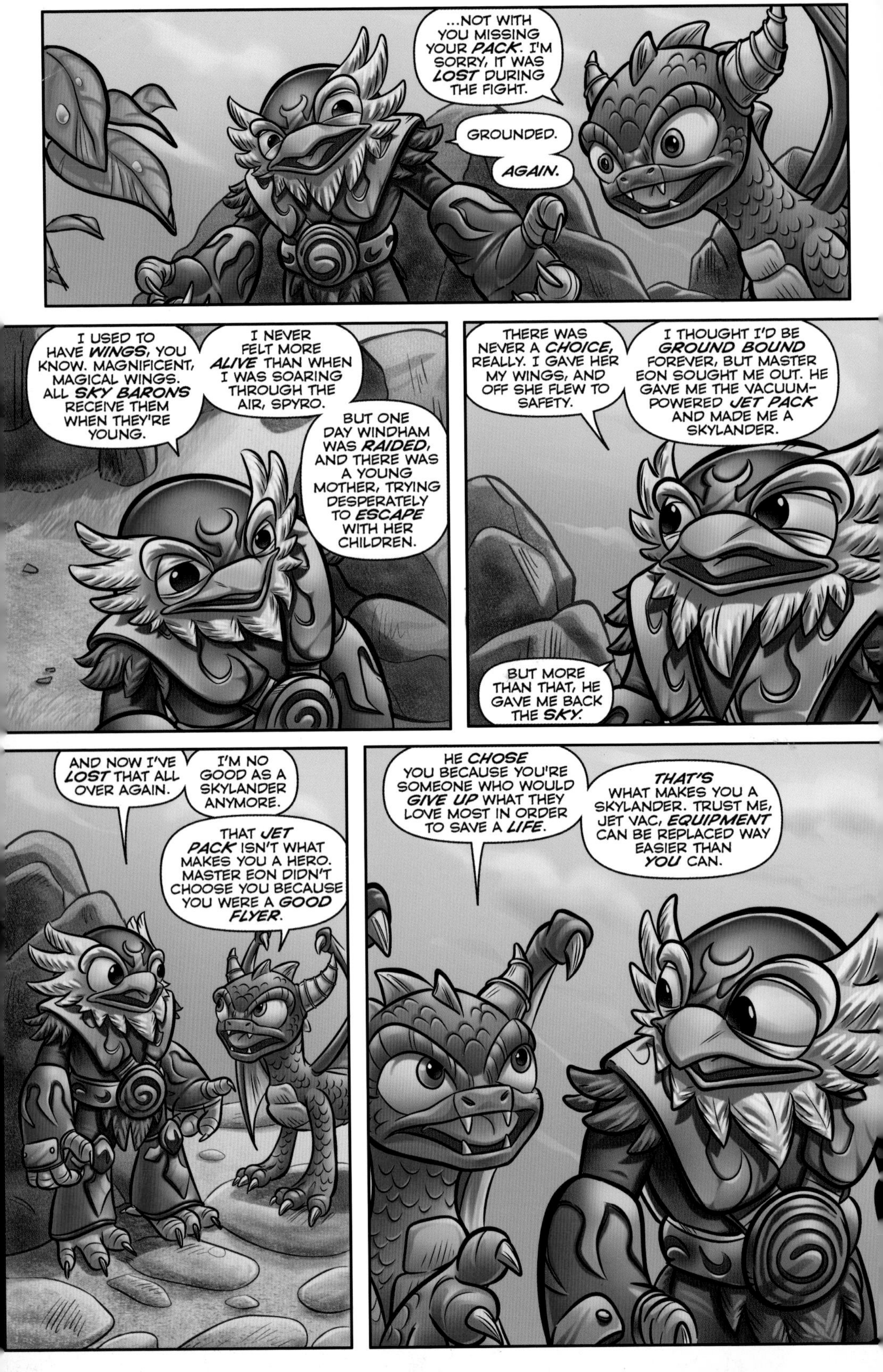
...NOT WITH YOU MISSING YOUR PACK. I'M SORRY, IT WAS LOST DURING THE FIGHT.
GROUNDED.
AGAIN.
I USED TO HAVE WINGS, YOU KNOW. MAGNIFICENT, MAGICAL WINGS. ALL SKY BARONS RECEIVE THEM WHEN THEY'RE YOUNG.
I NEVER FELT MORE ALIVE THAN WHEN I WAS SOARING THROUGH THE AIR, SPYRO.
BUT ONE DAY WINDHAM WAS RAIDED, AND THERE WAS A YOUNG MOTHER, TRYING DESPERATELY TO ESCAPE WITH HER CHILDREN.
THERE WAS NEVER A CHOICE, REALLY. I GAVE HER MY WINGS, AND OFF SHE FLEW TO SAFETY.
I THOUGHT I'D BE GROUND BOUND FOREVER, BUT MASTER EON SOUGHT ME OUT. HE GAVE ME THE VACUUM-POWERED JET PACK AND MADE ME A SKYLANDER.
BUT MORE THAN THAT, HE GAVE ME BACK THE SKY.
AND NOW I'VE LOST THAT ALL OVER AGAIN.
I'M NO GOOD AS A SKYLANDER ANYMORE.
THAT JET PACK ISN'T WHAT MAKES YOU A HERO. MASTER EON DIDN'T CHOOSE YOU BECAUSE YOU WERE A GOOD FLYER.
HE CHOSE YOU BECAUSE YOU'RE SOMEONE WHO WOULD GIVE UP WHAT THEY LOVE MOST IN ORDER TO SAVE A LIFE.
THAT'S WHAT MAKES YOU A SKYLANDER. TRUST ME, JET VAC, EQUIPMENT CAN BE REPLACED WAY EASIER THAN YOU CAN.

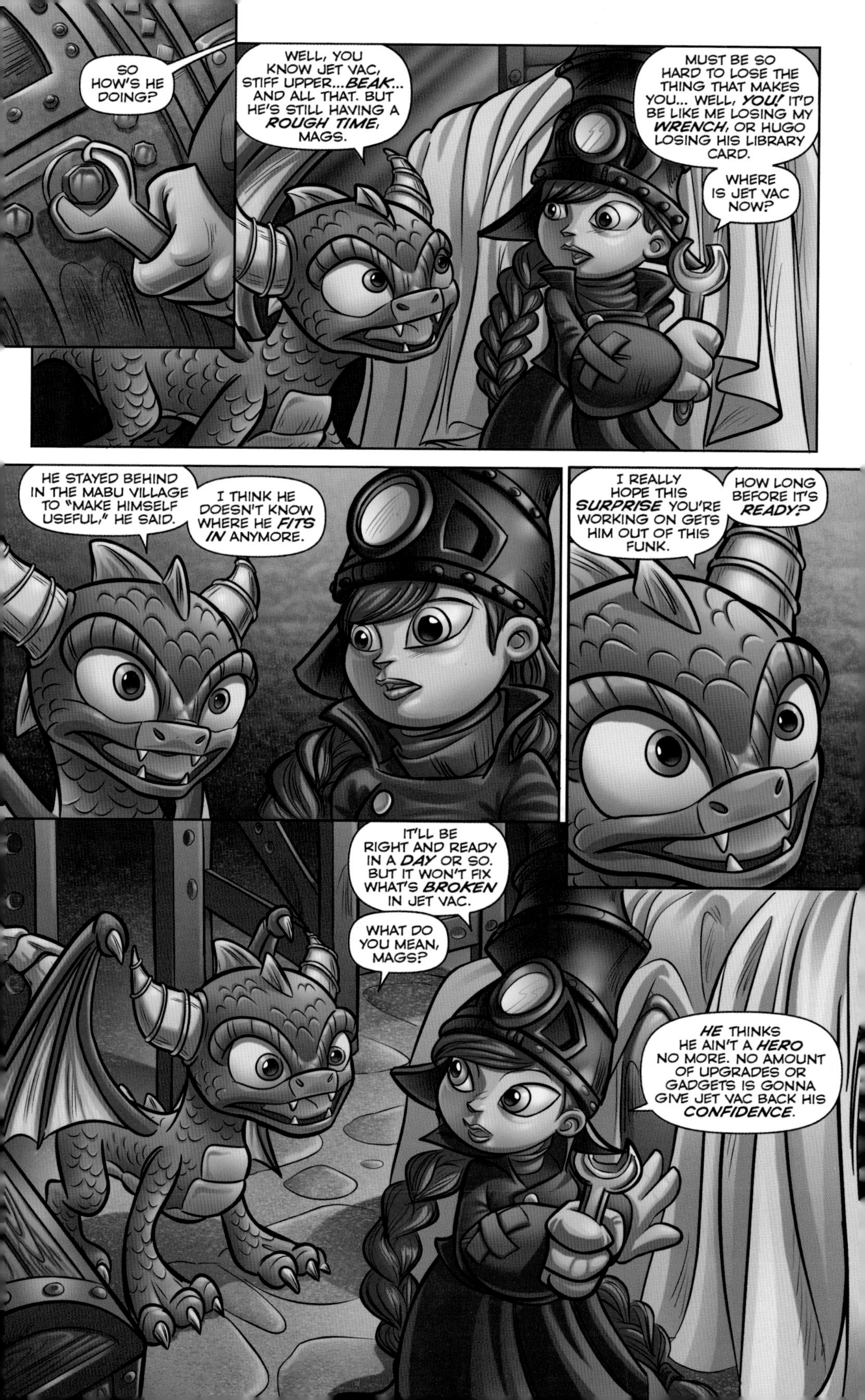
SO HOW'S HE DOING?
WELL, YOU KNOW JET VAC, STIFF UPPER...BEAK... AND ALL THAT. BUT HE'S STILL HAVING A ROUGH TIME, MAGS.
MUST BE SO HARD TO LOSE THE THING THAT MAKES YOU... WELL, YOU! IT'D BE LIKE ME LOSING MY WRENCH, OR HUGO LOSING HIS LIBRARY CARD.
WHERE IS JET VAC NOW?
HE STAYED BEHIND IN THE MABU VILLAGE TO "MAKE HIMSELF USEFUL," HE SAID.
I THINK HE DOESN'T KNOW WHERE HE FITS IN ANYMORE.
I REALLY HOPE THIS SURPRISE YOU'RE WORKING ON GETS HIM OUT OF THIS FUNK.
HOW LONG BEFORE IT'S READY?
IT'LL BE RIGHT AND READY IN A DAY OR SO. BUT IT WON'T FIX WHAT'S BROKEN IN JET VAC.
WHAT DO YOU MEAN, MAGS?
HE THINKS HE AIN'T A HERO NO MORE. NO AMOUNT OF UPGRADES OR GADGETS IS GONNA GIVE JET VAC BACK HIS CONFIDENCE.

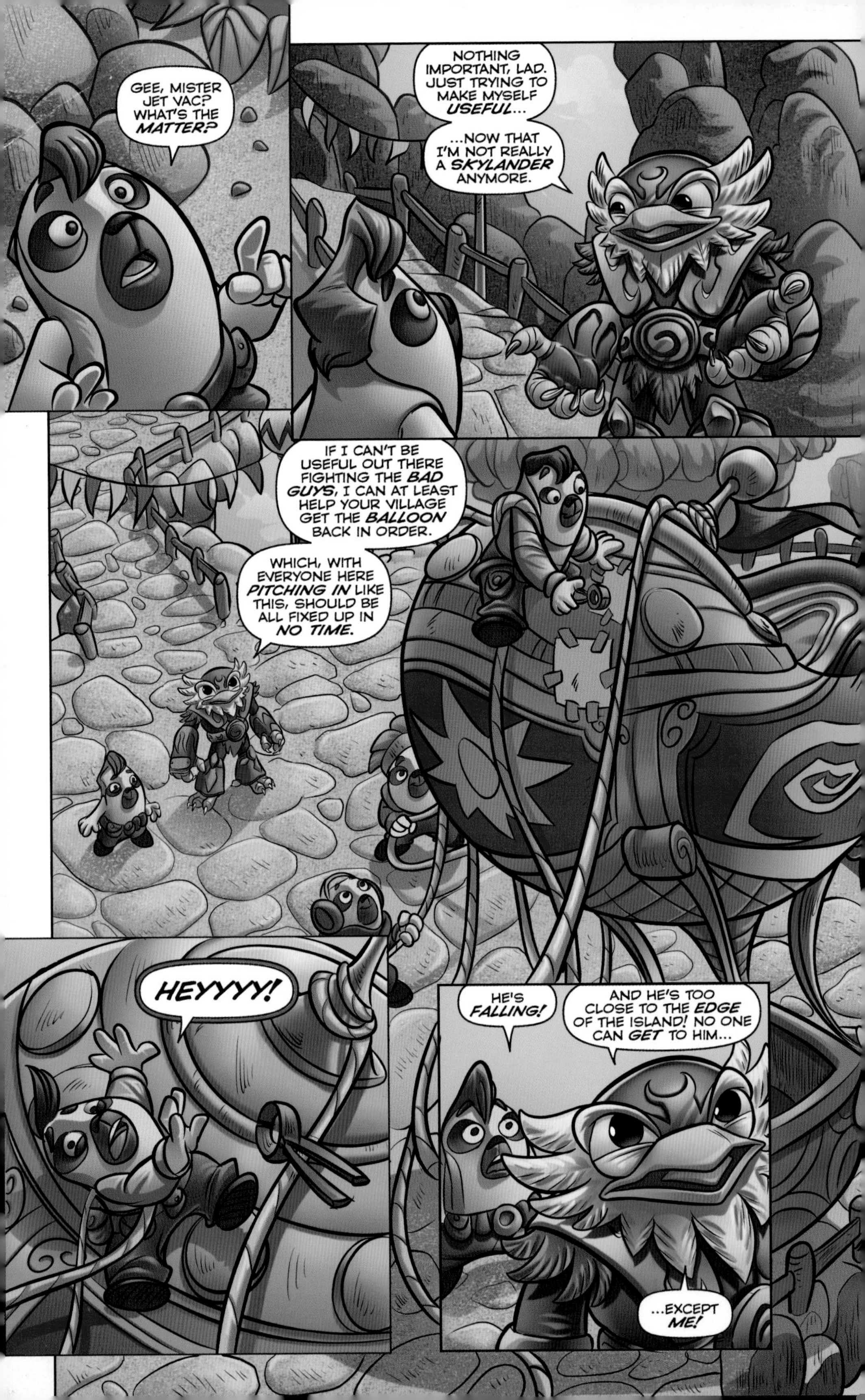
GEE, MISTER JET VAC? WHAT'S THE MATTER?
NOTHING IMPORTANT, LAD. JUST TRYING TO MAKE MYSELF USEFUL...
...NOW THAT I'M NOT REALLY A SKYLANDER ANYMORE.
IF I CAN'T BE USEFUL OUT THERE FIGHTING THE BAD GUYS, I CAN AT LEAST HELP YOUR VILLAGE GET THE BALLOON BACK IN ORDER.
WHICH, WITH EVERYONE HERE PITCHING IN LIKE THIS, SHOULD BE ALL FIXED UP IN NO TIME.
HEYYYY!
HE'S FALLING!
AND HE'S TOO CLOSE TO THE EDGE OF THE ISLAND! NO ONE CAN GET TO HIM...
...EXCEPT ME!

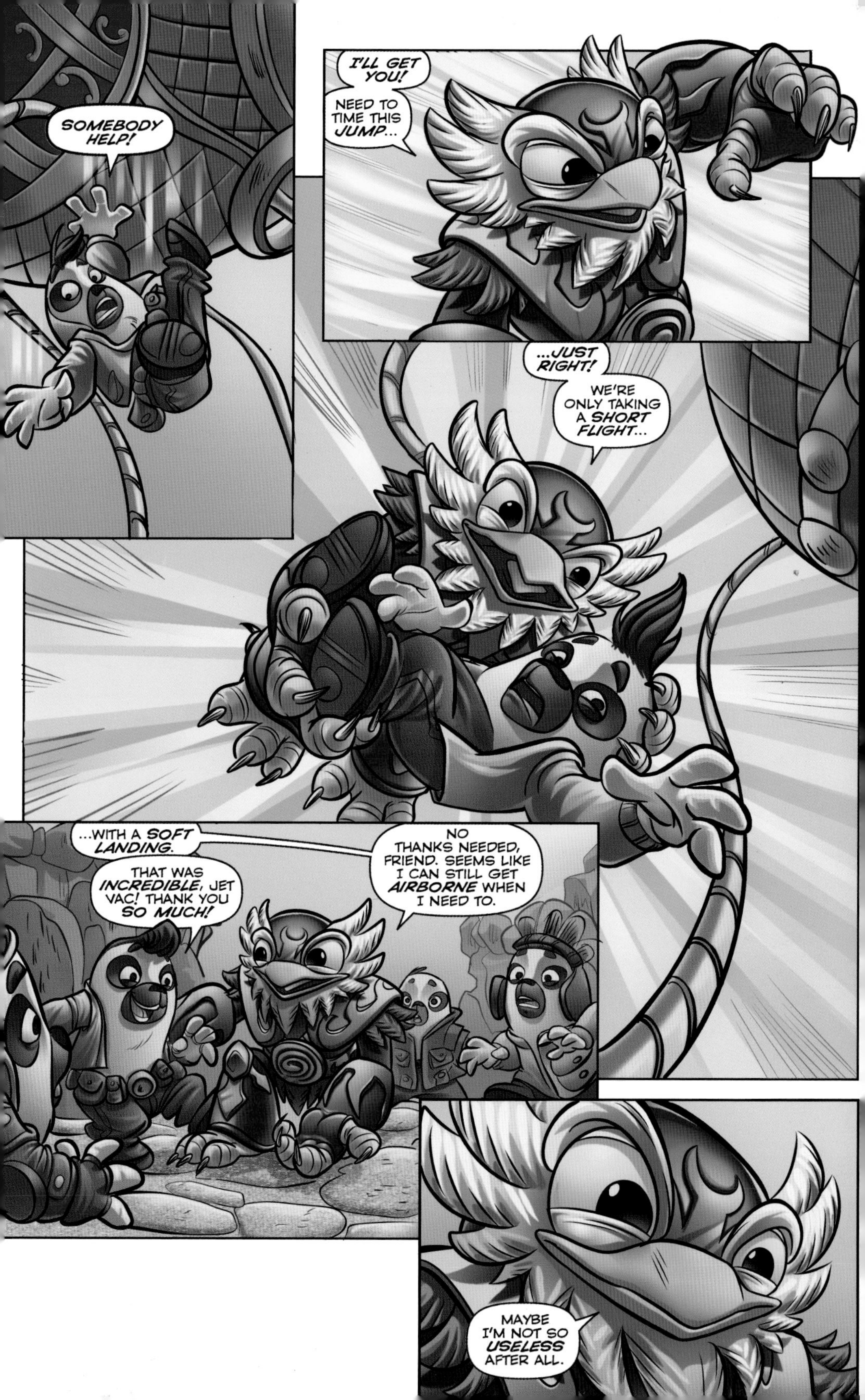

SOMEBODY HELP!
I'LL GET YOU!
NEED TO TIME THIS JUMP...
...JUST RIGHT!
WE'RE ONLY TAKING A SHORT FLIGHT...
...WITH A SOFT LANDING.
THAT WAS INCREDIBLE, JET VAC! THANK YOU SO MUCH!
NO THANKS NEEDED, FRIEND. SEEMS LIKE I CAN STILL GET AIRBORNE WHEN I NEED TO.
MAYBE I'M NOT SO USELESS AFTER ALL.

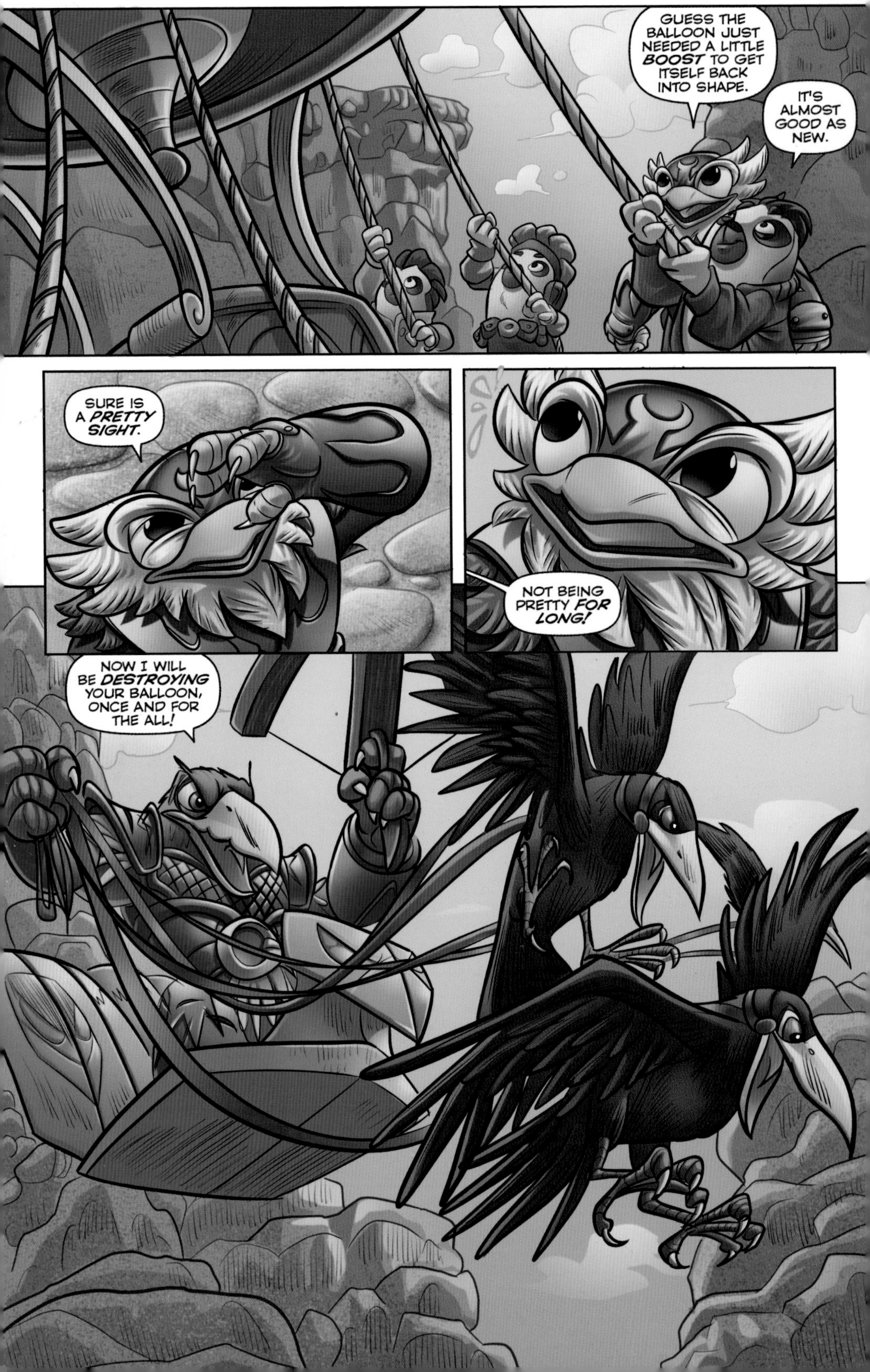
GUESS THE BALLOON JUST NEEDED A LITTLE BOOST TO GET ITSELF BACK INTO SHAPE.
IT'S ALMOST GOOD AS NEW.
SURE IS A PRETTY SIGHT.
NOT BEING PRETTY FOR LONG!
NOW I WILL BE DESTROYING YOUR BALLOON, ONCE AND FOR THE ALL!

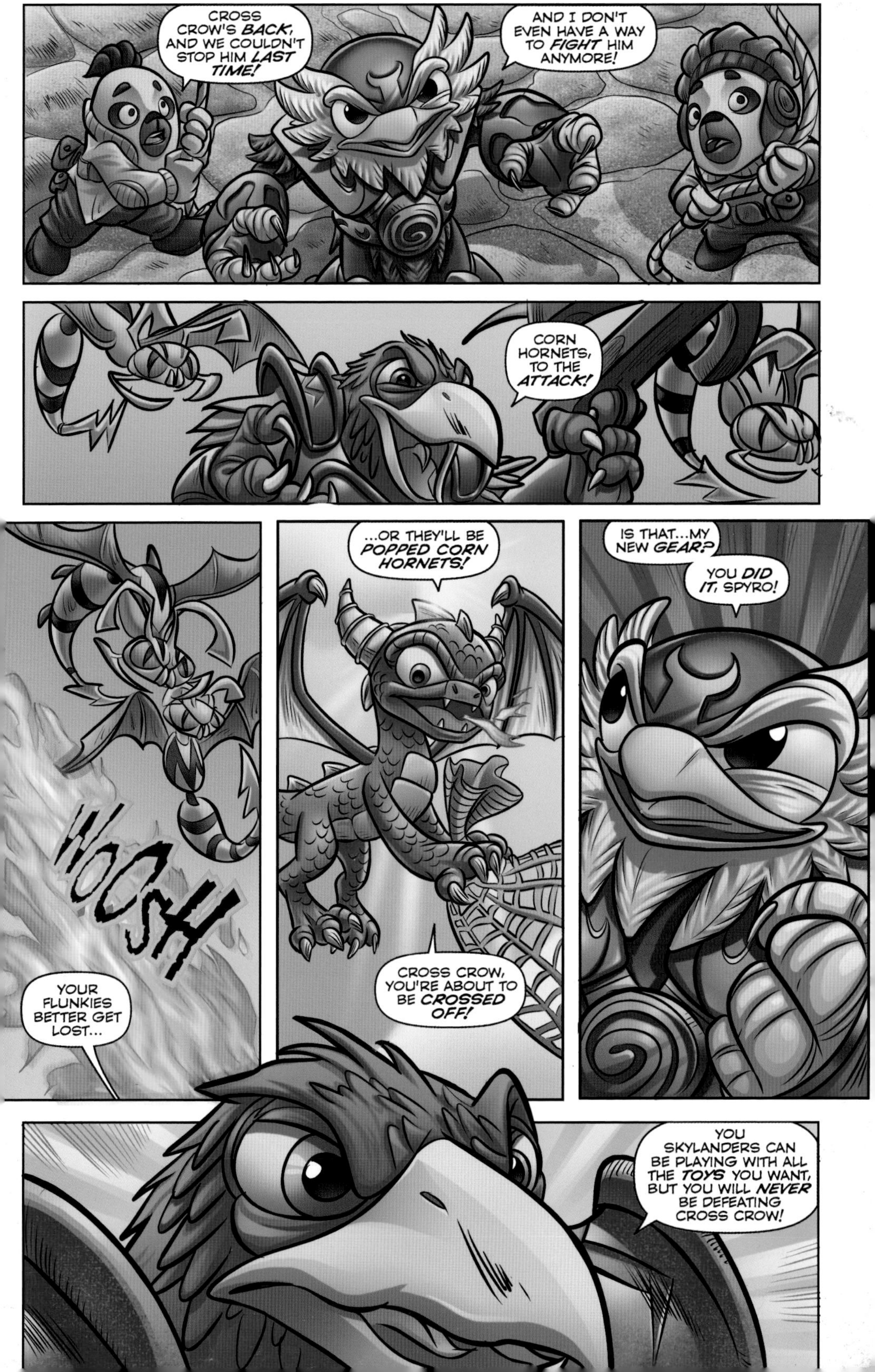
CROSS CROW'S BACK, AND WE COULDN'T STOP HIM LAST TIME!
AND I DON'T EVEN HAVE A WAY TO FIGHT HIM ANYMORE!
CORN HORNETS, TO THE ATTACK!
HOOSH
YOUR FLUNKIES BETTER GET LOST...
...OR THEY'LL BE POPPED CORN HORNETS!
CROSS CROW, YOU'RE ABOUT TO BE CROSSED OFF!
IS THAT...MY NEW GEAR?
YOU DID IT, SPYRO!
YOU SKYLANDERS CAN BE PLAYING WITH ALL THE TOYS YOU WANT, BUT YOU WILL NEVER BE DEFEATING CROSS CROW!

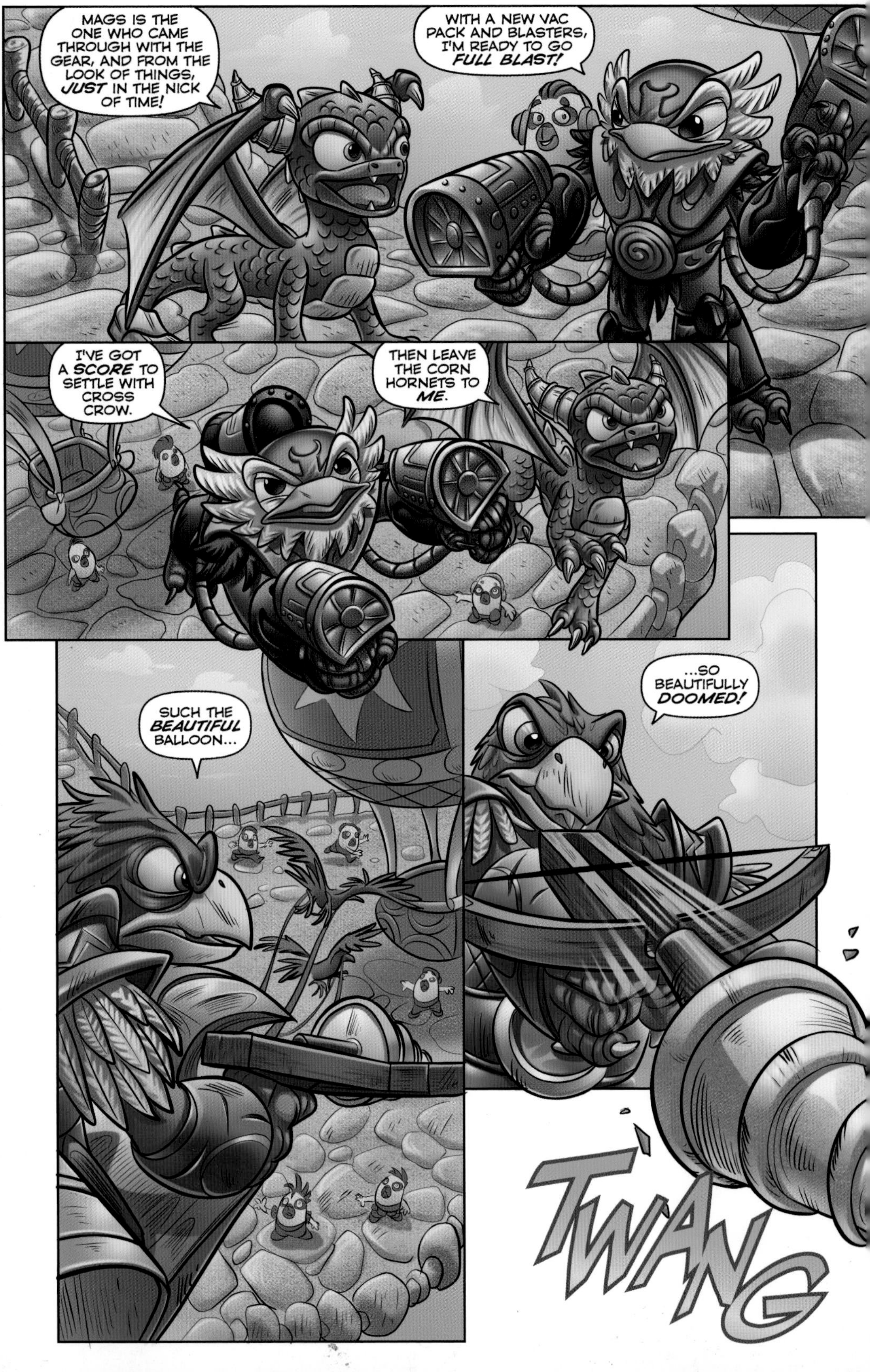
MAGS IS THE ONE WHO CAME THROUGH WITH THE GEAR, AND FROM THE LOOK OF THINGS, *JUST* IN THE NICK OF TIME!
WITH A NEW VAC PACK AND BLASTERS, I'M READY TO GO *FULL BLAST!*
I'VE GOT A *SCORE* TO SETTLE WITH CROSS CROW.
THEN LEAVE THE CORN HORNETS TO *ME*.
SUCH THE *BEAUTIFUL* BALLOON...
...SO BEAUTIFULLY *DOOMED!*
TWANG

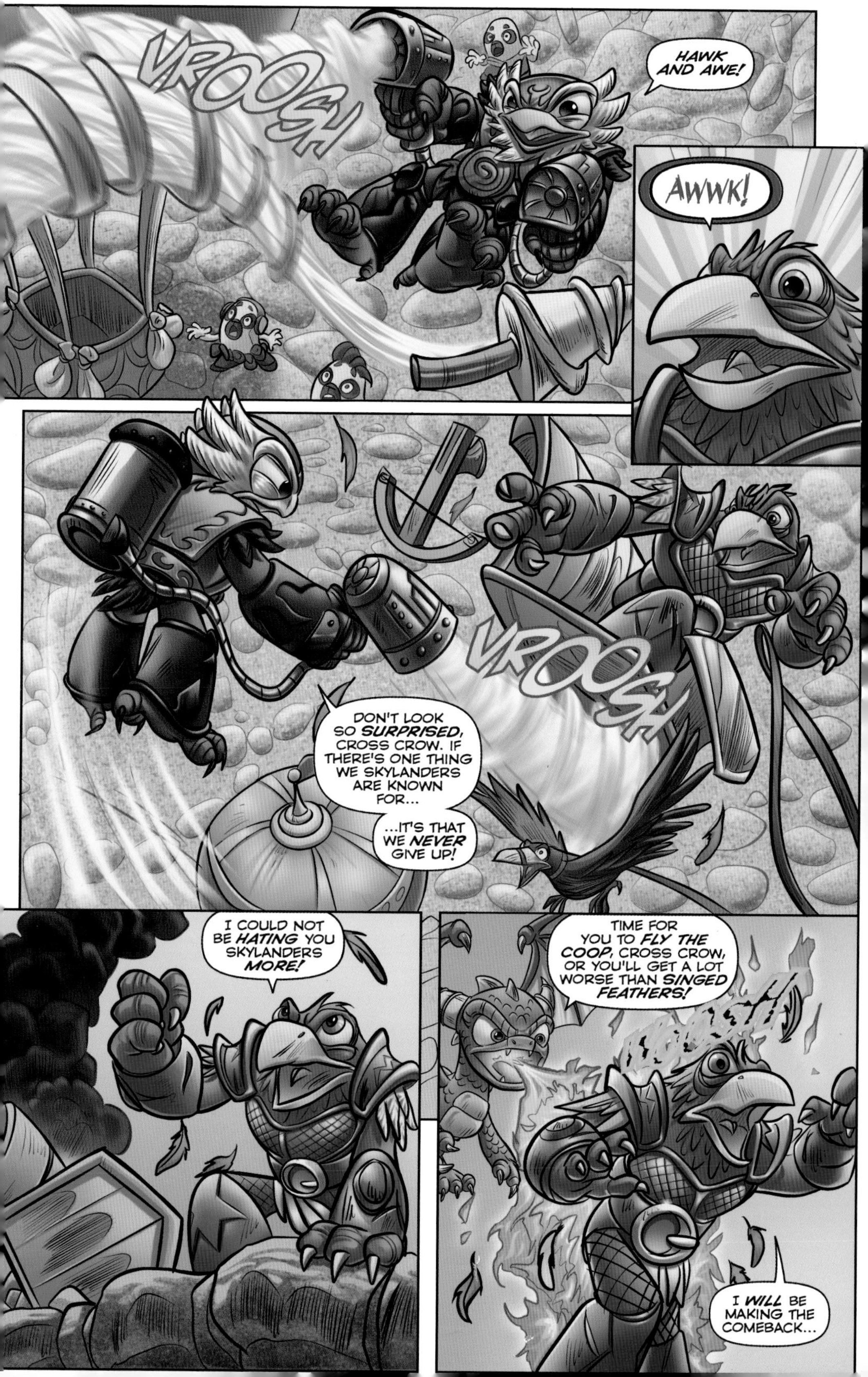
VROOSH!
HAWK AND AWE!
AWWK!
VROOSH
DON'T LOOK SO SURPRISED, CROSS CROW. IF THERE'S ONE THING WE SKYLANDERS ARE KNOWN FOR...
...IT'S THAT WE NEVER GIVE UP!
I COULD NOT BE HATING YOU SKYLANDERS MORE!
TIME FOR YOU TO FLY THE COOP, CROSS CROW, OR YOU'LL GET A LOT WORSE THAN SINGED FEATHERS!
I WILL BE MAKING THE COMEBACK...

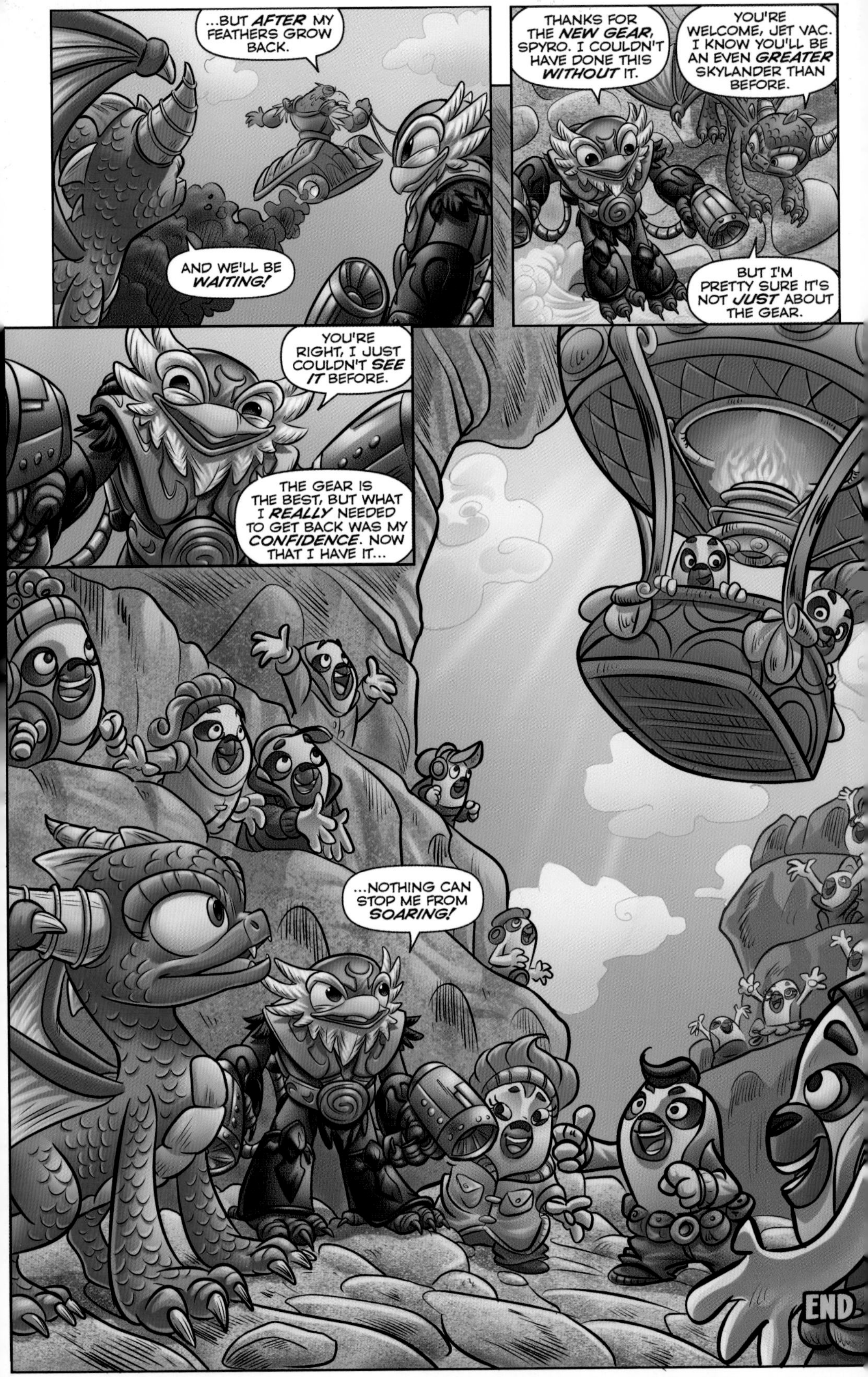
...BUT AFTER MY FEATHERS GROW BACK.
AND WE'LL BE WAITING!
THANKS FOR THE NEW GEAR, SPYRO. I COULDN'T HAVE DONE THIS WITHOUT IT.
YOU'RE WELCOME, JET VAC. I KNOW YOU'LL BE AN EVEN GREATER SKYLANDER THAN BEFORE.
BUT I'M PRETTY SURE IT'S NOT JUST ABOUT THE GEAR.
YOU'RE RIGHT, I JUST COULDN'T SEE IT BEFORE.
THE GEAR IS THE BEST, BUT WHAT I REALLY NEEDED TO GET BACK WAS MY CONFIDENCE. NOW THAT I HAVE IT...
...NOTHING CAN STOP ME FROM SOARING!
END

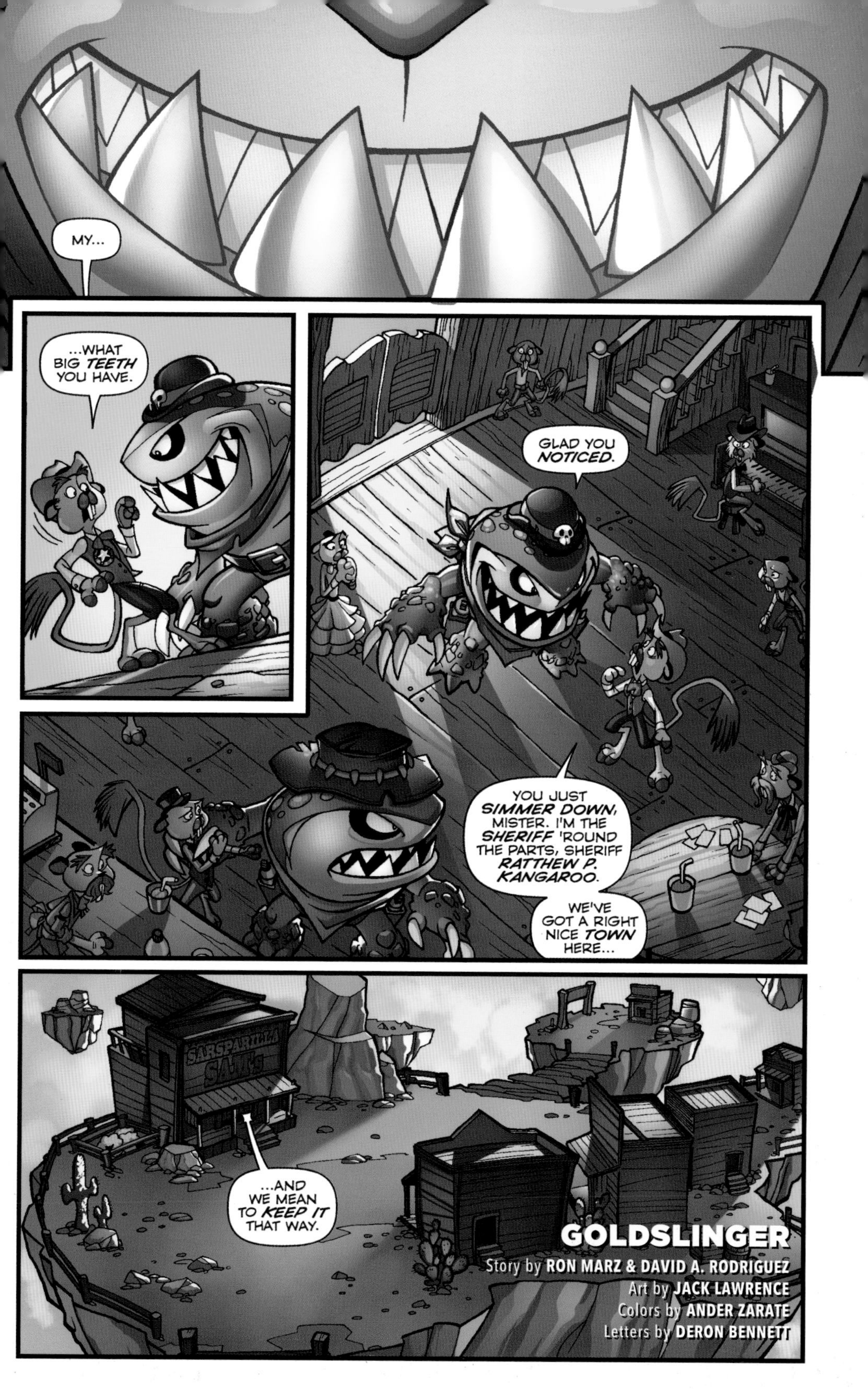
MY...
...WHAT BIG *TEETH* YOU HAVE.
GLAD YOU *NOTICED*.
YOU JUST *SIMMER DOWN*, MISTER. I'M THE *SHERIFF* 'ROUND THE PARTS, SHERIFF *RATTHEW P. KANGAROO*.
WE'VE GOT A RIGHT NICE *TOWN* HERE...
...AND WE MEAN TO *KEEP IT* THAT WAY.
GOLDSLINGER
Story by RON MARZ & DAVID A. RODRIGUEZ
Art by JACK LAWRENCE
Colors by ANDER ZARATE
Letters by DERON BENNETT

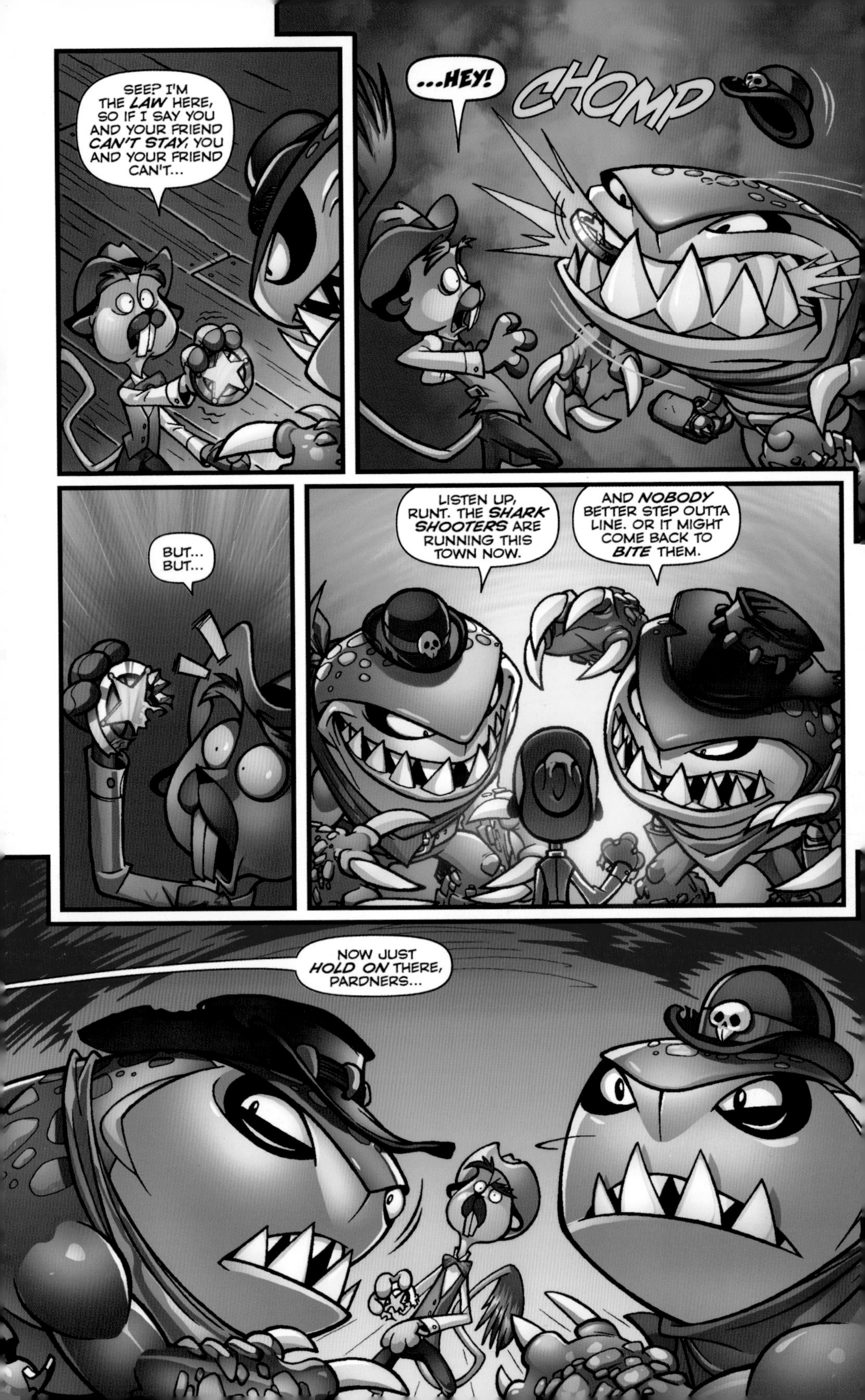
SEE? I'M THE LAW HERE, SO IF I SAY YOU AND YOUR FRIEND CAN'T STAY, YOU AND YOUR FRIEND CAN'T...
...HEY!
CHOMP
BUT... BUT...
LISTEN UP, RUNT. THE SHARK SHOOTERS ARE RUNNING THIS TOWN NOW.
AND NOBODY BETTER STEP OUTTA LINE. OR IT MIGHT COME BACK TO BITE THEM.
NOW JUST HOLD ON THERE, PARDNERS...

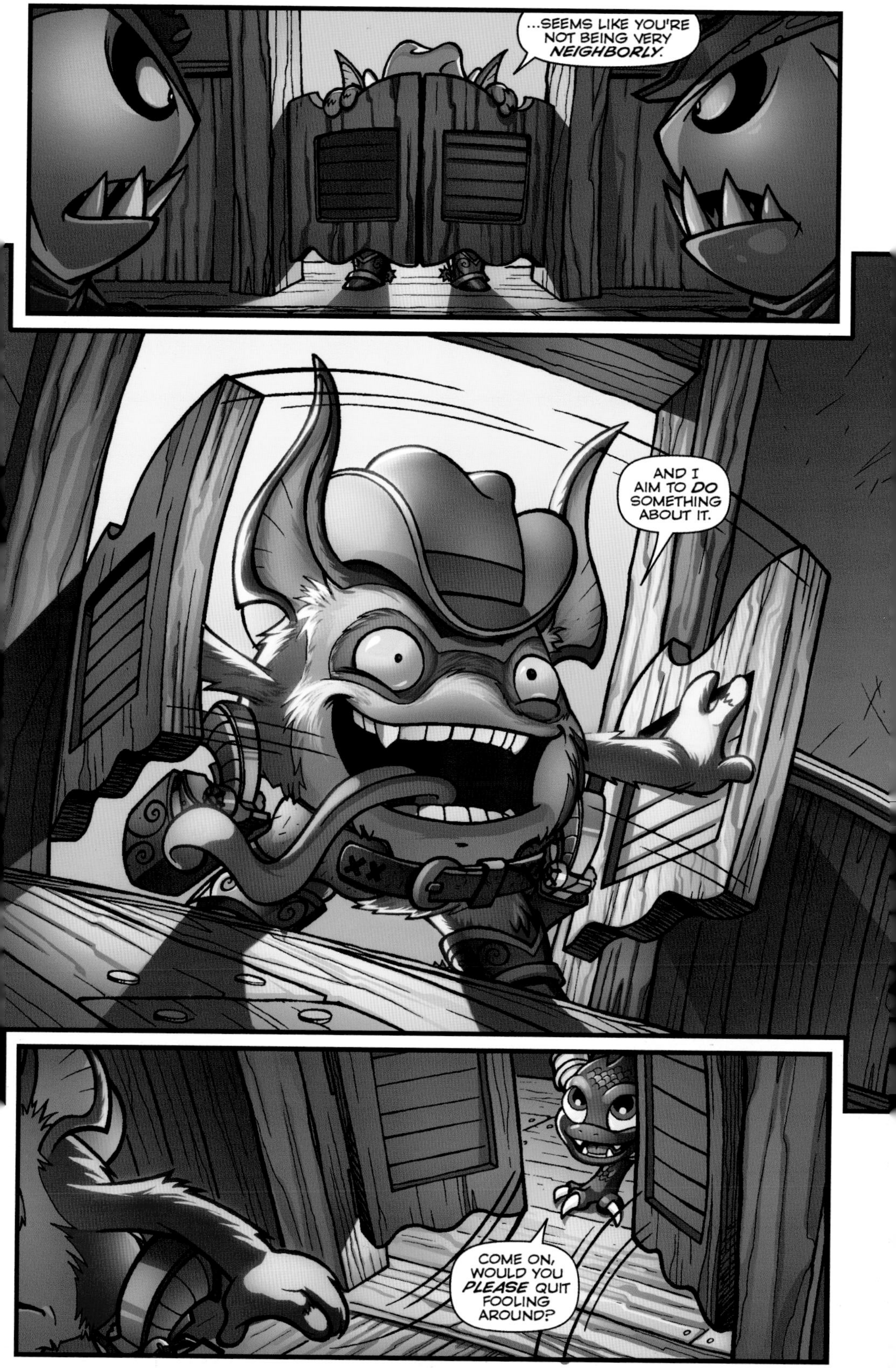
...SEEMS LIKE YOU'RE NOT BEING VERY *NEIGHBORLY*.
AND I AIM TO *DO* SOMETHING ABOUT IT.
COME ON, WOULD YOU *PLEASE* QUIT FOOLING AROUND?

SAM'S

WHO ARE *YOU* SUPPOSED TO BE?

HAPPY...

TOONG

SPÚTT

...*TRIGGER HAPPY*.

AND THIS HERE'S MY PARTNER, THE *SPYRO KID*.

*JUST* SPYRO IS FINE.

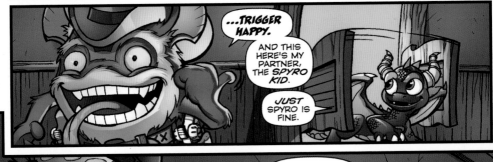

NOW WE'RE GIVING YOU BOYS *ONE CHANCE* TO MOSEY ON OUTTA TOWN AND *NEVER* COME BACK.

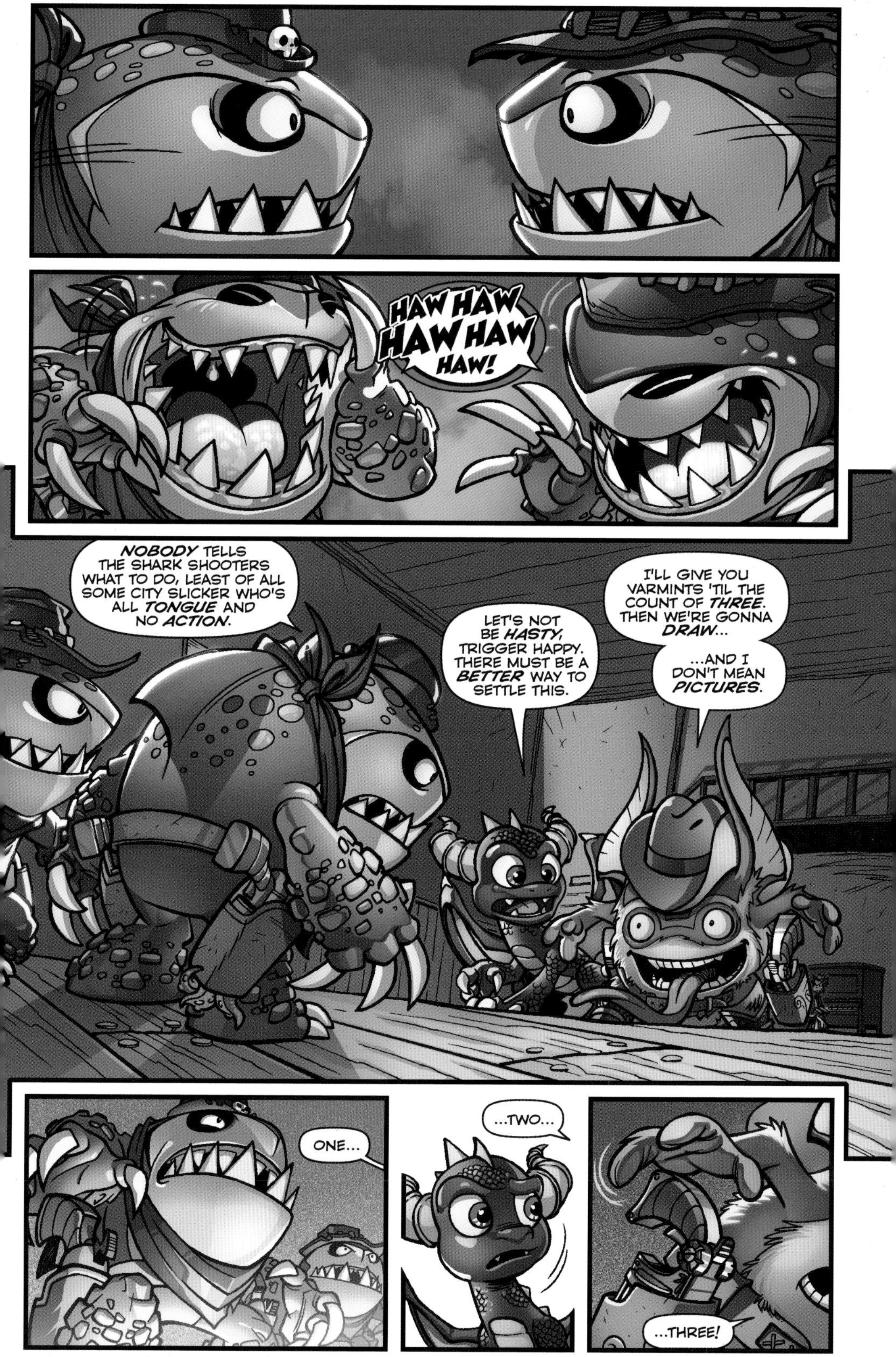
HAW HAW HAW HAW HAW!
NOBODY TELLS THE SHARK SHOOTERS WHAT TO DO, LEAST OF ALL SOME CITY SLICKER WHO'S ALL TONGUE AND NO ACTION.
LET'S NOT BE HASTY, TRIGGER HAPPY. THERE MUST BE A BETTER WAY TO SETTLE THIS.
I'LL GIVE YOU VARMINTS 'TIL THE COUNT OF THREE. THEN WE'RE GONNA DRAW...
...AND I DON'T MEAN PICTURES.
ONE...
...TWO...
...THREE!

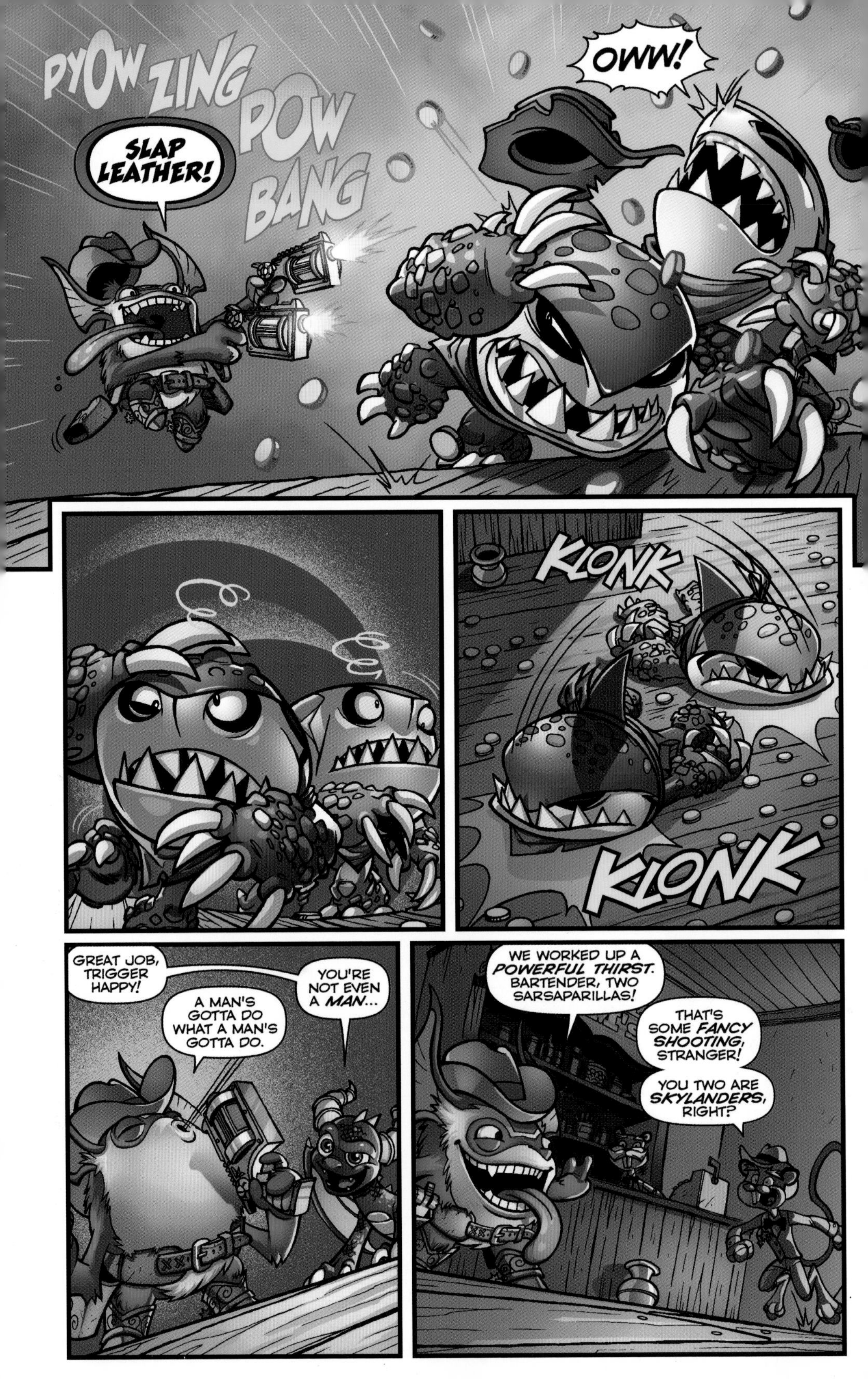
PYOW ZING POW BANG
SLAP LEATHER!
OWW!
KLONK
KLONK
GREAT JOB, TRIGGER HAPPY!
YOU'RE NOT EVEN A *MAN*...
A MAN'S GOTTA DO WHAT A MAN'S GOTTA DO.
WE WORKED UP A *POWERFUL THIRST*. BARTENDER, TWO SARSAPARILLAS!
THAT'S SOME *FANCY SHOOTING*, STRANGER!
YOU TWO ARE *SKYLANDERS*, RIGHT?

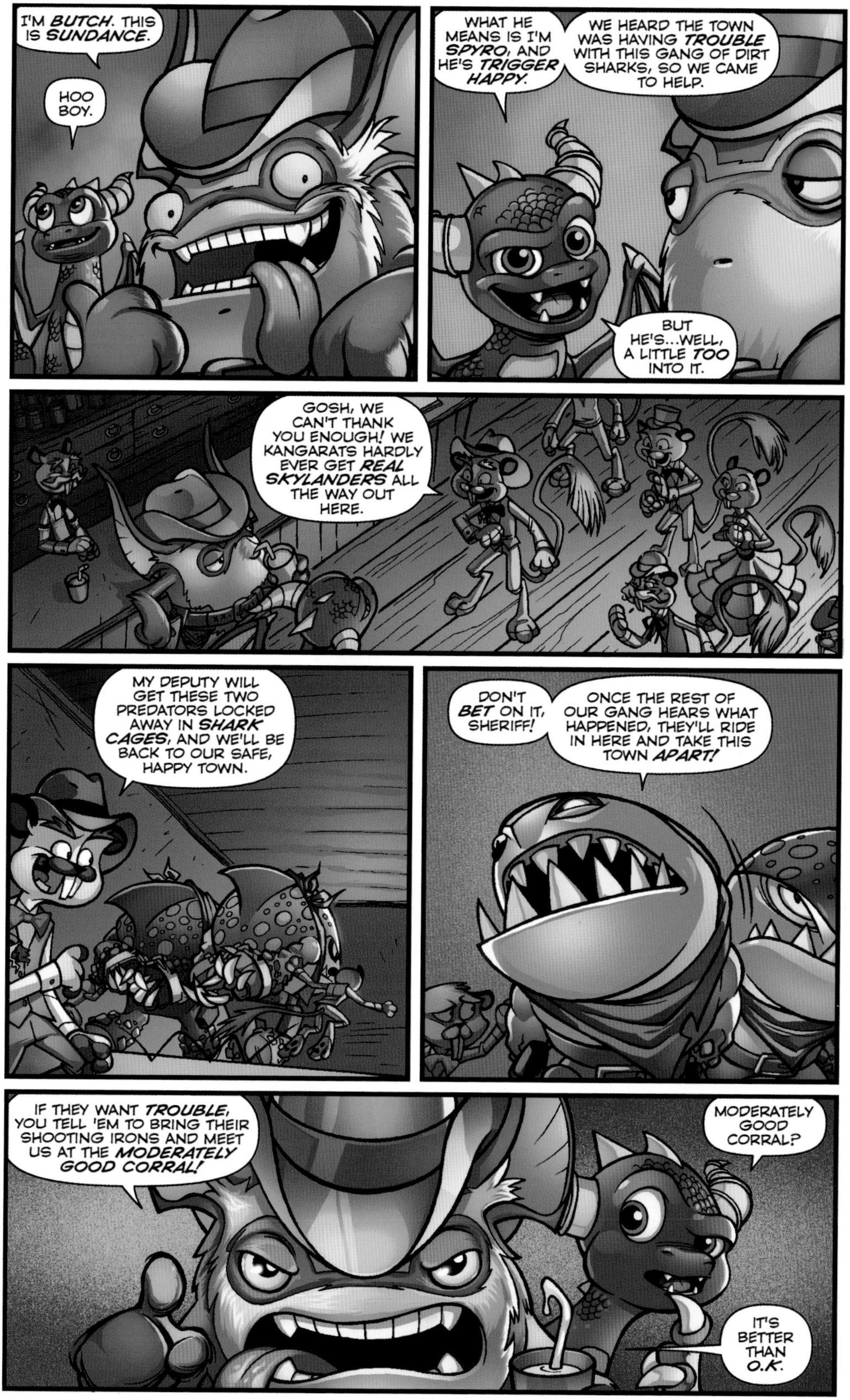
I'M BUTCH. THIS IS SUNDANCE.
HOO BOY.
WHAT HE MEANS IS I'M SPYRO, AND HE'S TRIGGER HAPPY.
WE HEARD THE TOWN WAS HAVING TROUBLE WITH THIS GANG OF DIRT SHARKS, SO WE CAME TO HELP.
BUT HE'S...WELL, A LITTLE TOO INTO IT.
GOSH, WE CAN'T THANK YOU ENOUGH! WE KANGARATS HARDLY EVER GET REAL SKYLANDERS ALL THE WAY OUT HERE.
MY DEPUTY WILL GET THESE TWO PREDATORS LOCKED AWAY IN SHARK CAGES, AND WE'LL BE BACK TO OUR SAFE, HAPPY TOWN.
DON'T BET ON IT, SHERIFF!
ONCE THE REST OF OUR GANG HEARS WHAT HAPPENED, THEY'LL RIDE IN HERE AND TAKE THIS TOWN APART!
IF THEY WANT TROUBLE, YOU TELL 'EM TO BRING THEIR SHOOTING IRONS AND MEET US AT THE MODERATELY GOOD CORRAL!
MODERATELY GOOD CORRAL?
IT'S BETTER THAN O.K.

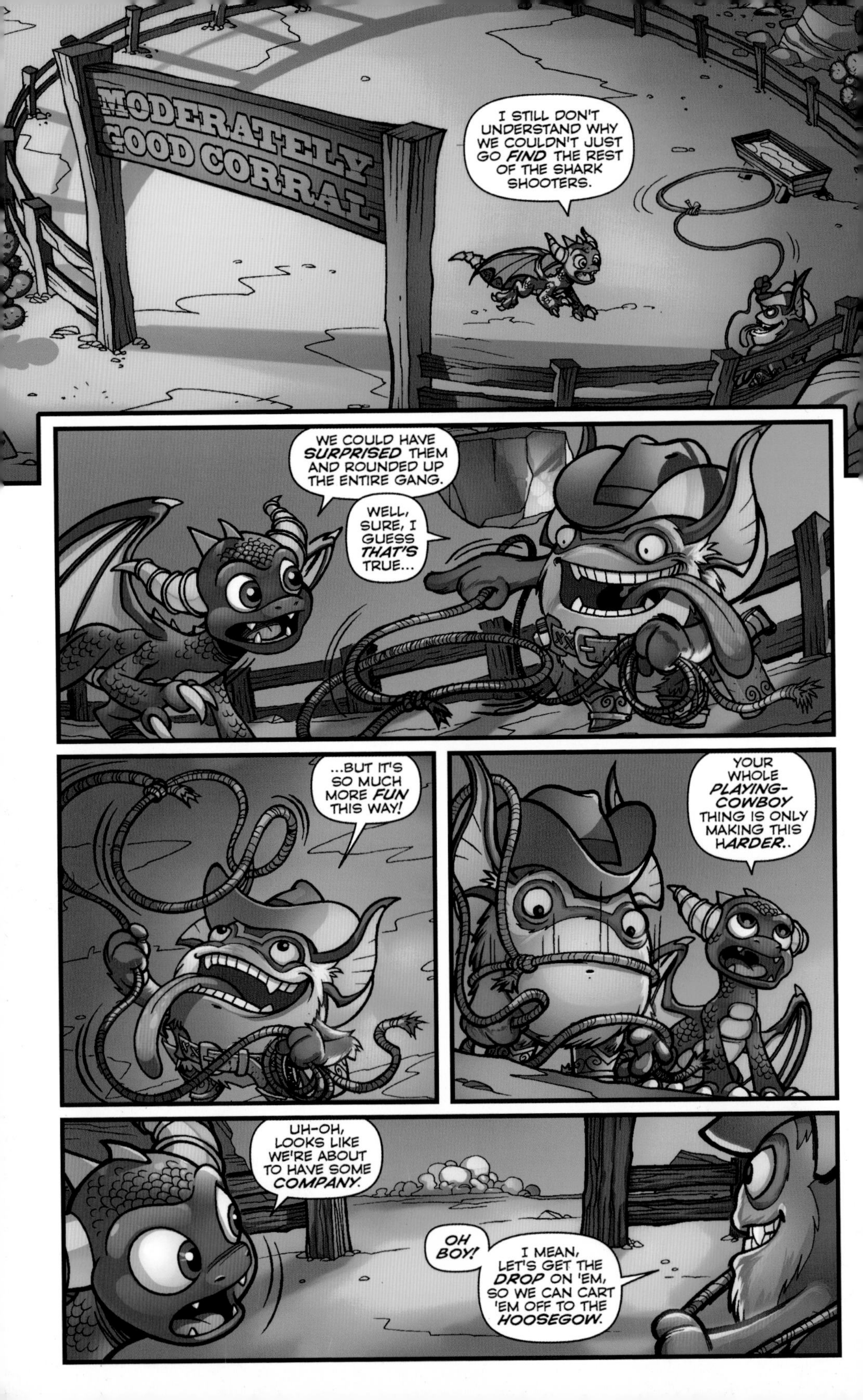
MODERATELY GOOD CORRAL
I STILL DON'T UNDERSTAND WHY WE COULDN'T JUST GO FIND THE REST OF THE SHARK SHOOTERS.
WE COULD HAVE SURPRISED THEM AND ROUNDED UP THE ENTIRE GANG.
WELL, SURE, I GUESS THAT'S TRUE...
...BUT IT'S SO MUCH MORE FUN THIS WAY!
YOUR WHOLE PLAYING-COWBOY THING IS ONLY MAKING THIS HARDER..
UH-OH, LOOKS LIKE WE'RE ABOUT TO HAVE SOME COMPANY.
OH BOY!
I MEAN, LET'S GET THE DROP ON 'EM, SO WE CAN CART 'EM OFF TO THE HOOSEGOW.

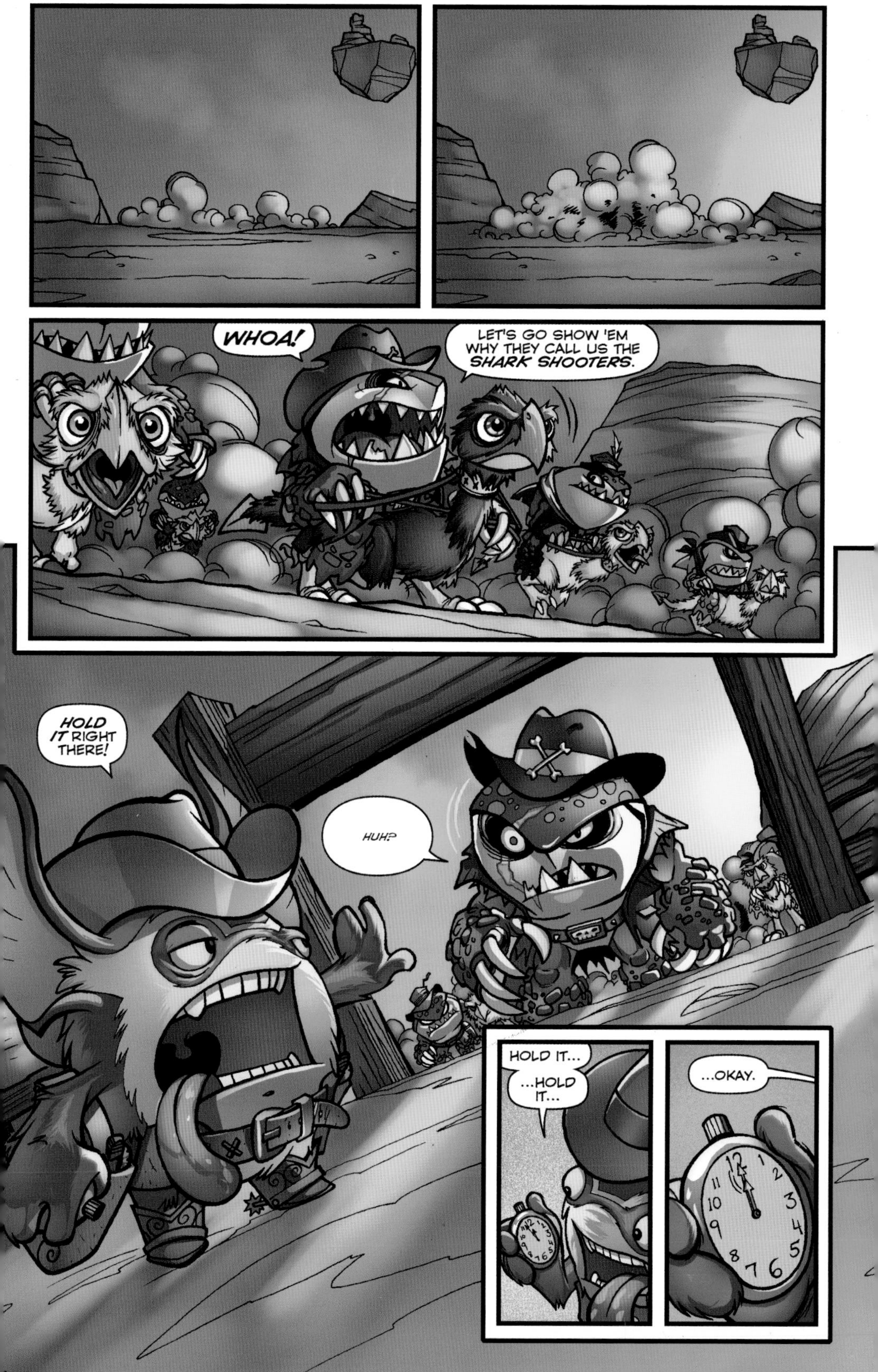
WHOA!
LET'S GO SHOW 'EM WHY THEY CALL US THE SHARK SHOOTERS.
HOLD IT RIGHT THERE!
HUH?
HOLD IT...
...HOLD IT...
...OKAY.

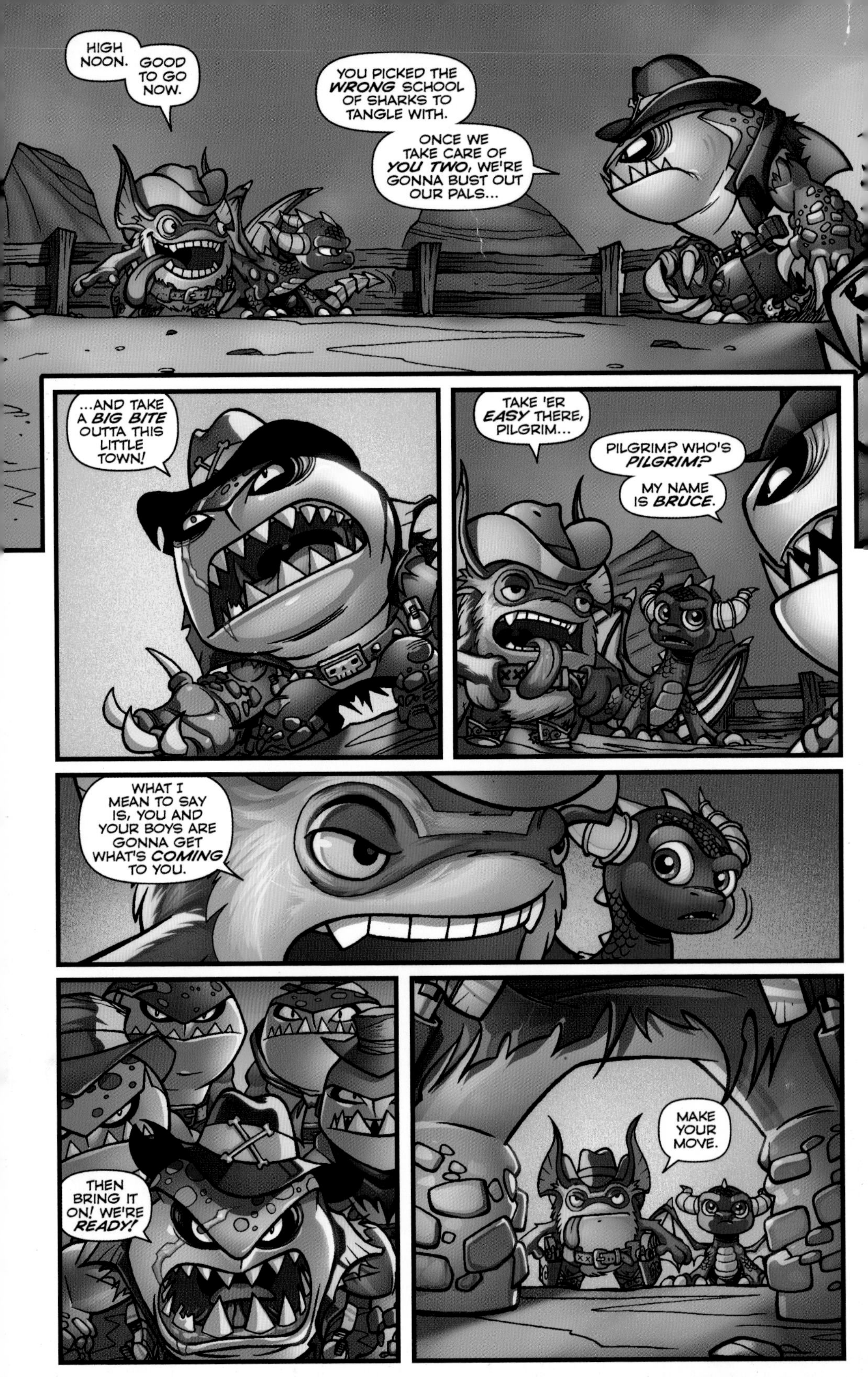
HIGH NOON. GOOD TO GO NOW.
YOU PICKED THE WRONG SCHOOL OF SHARKS TO TANGLE WITH.
ONCE WE TAKE CARE OF YOU TWO, WE'RE GONNA BUST OUT OUR PALS...
...AND TAKE A BIG BITE OUTTA THIS LITTLE TOWN!
TAKE 'ER EASY THERE, PILGRIM...
PILGRIM? WHO'S PILGRIM?
MY NAME IS BRUCE.
WHAT I MEAN TO SAY IS, YOU AND YOUR BOYS ARE GONNA GET WHAT'S COMING TO YOU.
THEN BRING IT ON! WE'RE READY!
MAKE YOUR MOVE.

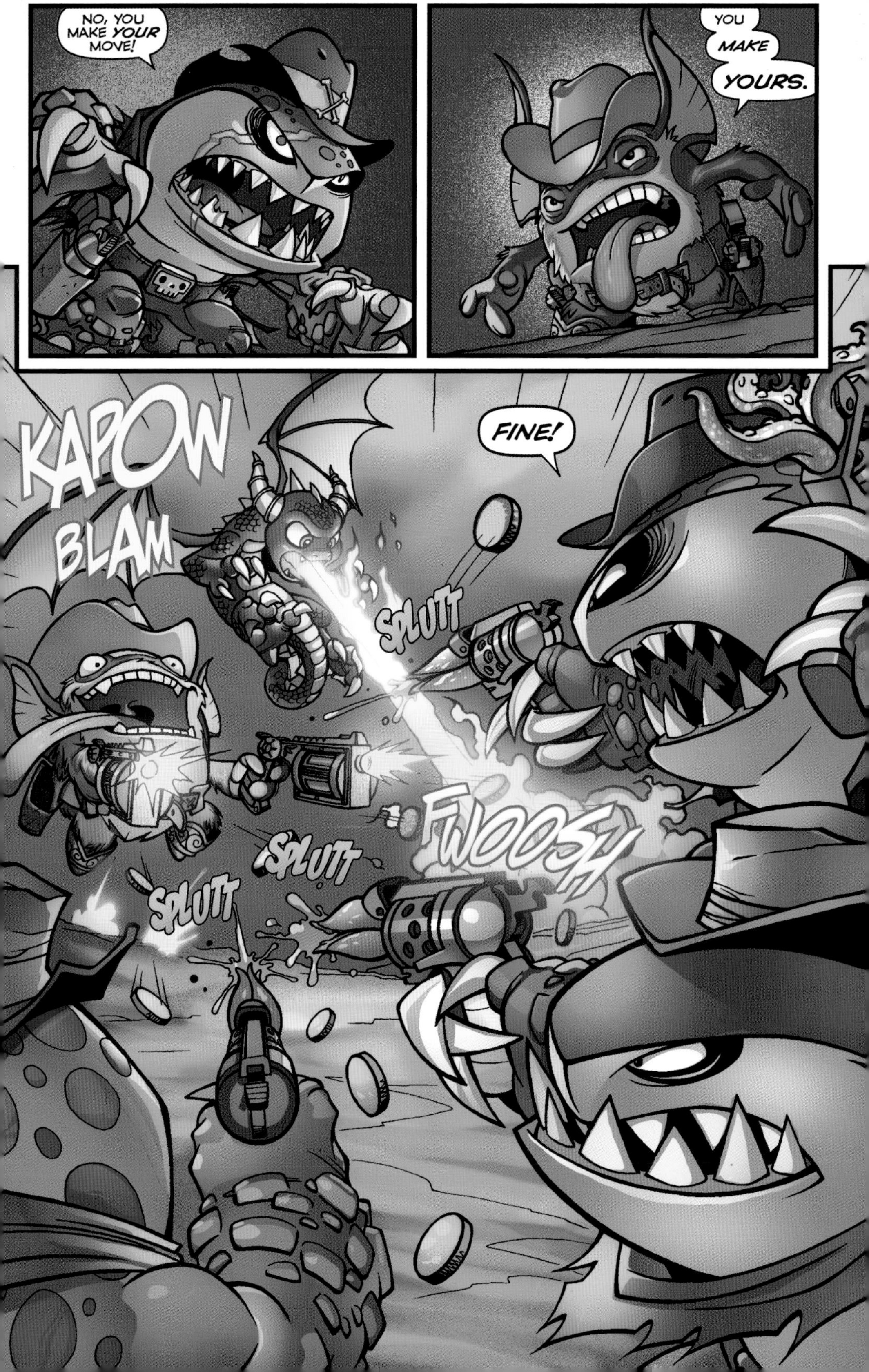
NO, YOU MAKE *YOUR* MOVE!
YOU *MAKE* YOURS.
KAPOW
BLAM
FINE!
SPLUTT
FWOOSH
SPLUTT
SPLUTT

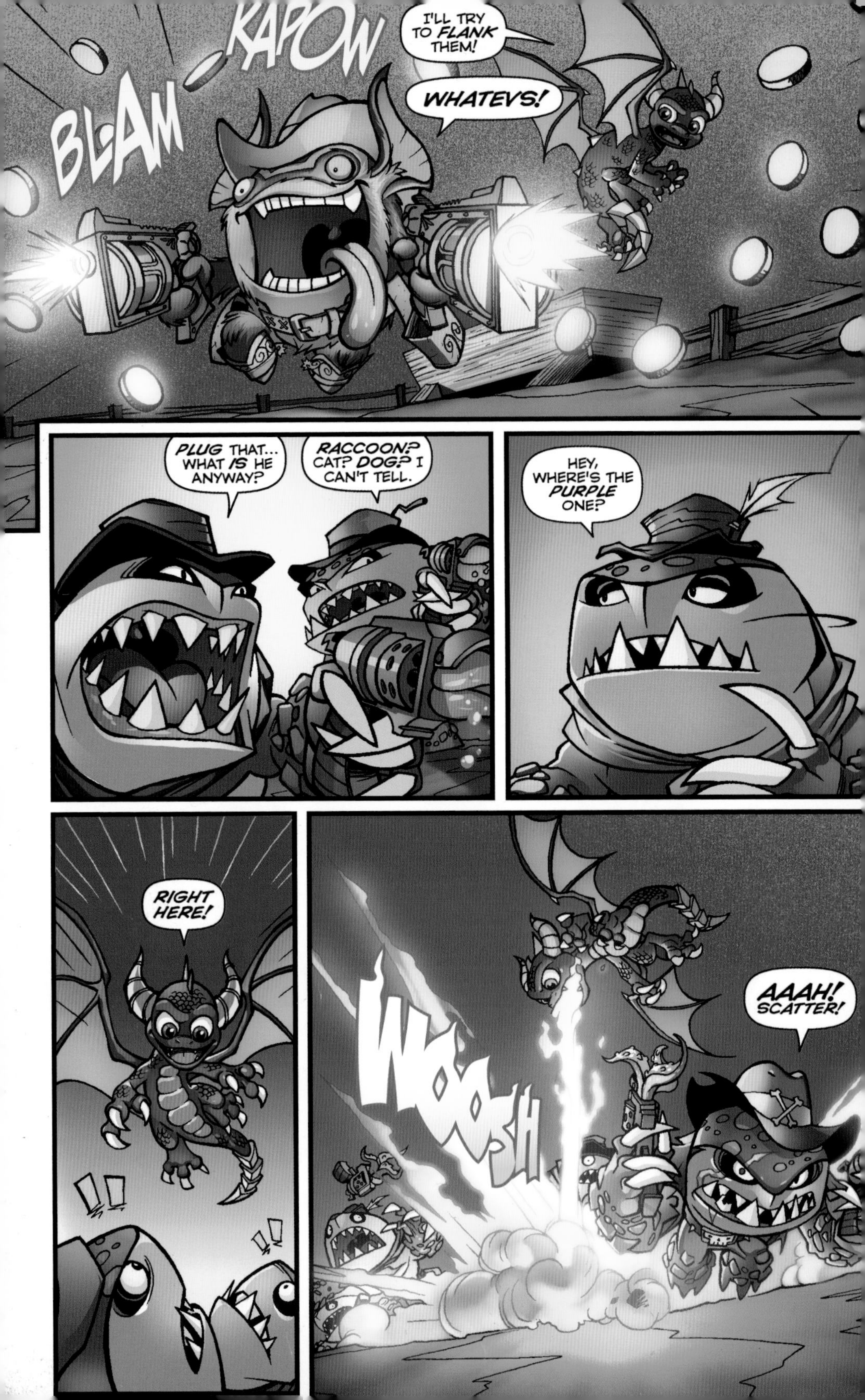
BLAM
KAPOW
I'LL TRY TO FLANK THEM!
WHATEVS!
PLUG THAT... WHAT IS HE ANYWAY?
RACCOON? CAT? DOG? I CAN'T TELL.
HEY, WHERE'S THE PURPLE ONE?
RIGHT HERE!
!!
!!
WOOSH
AAAH! SCATTER!

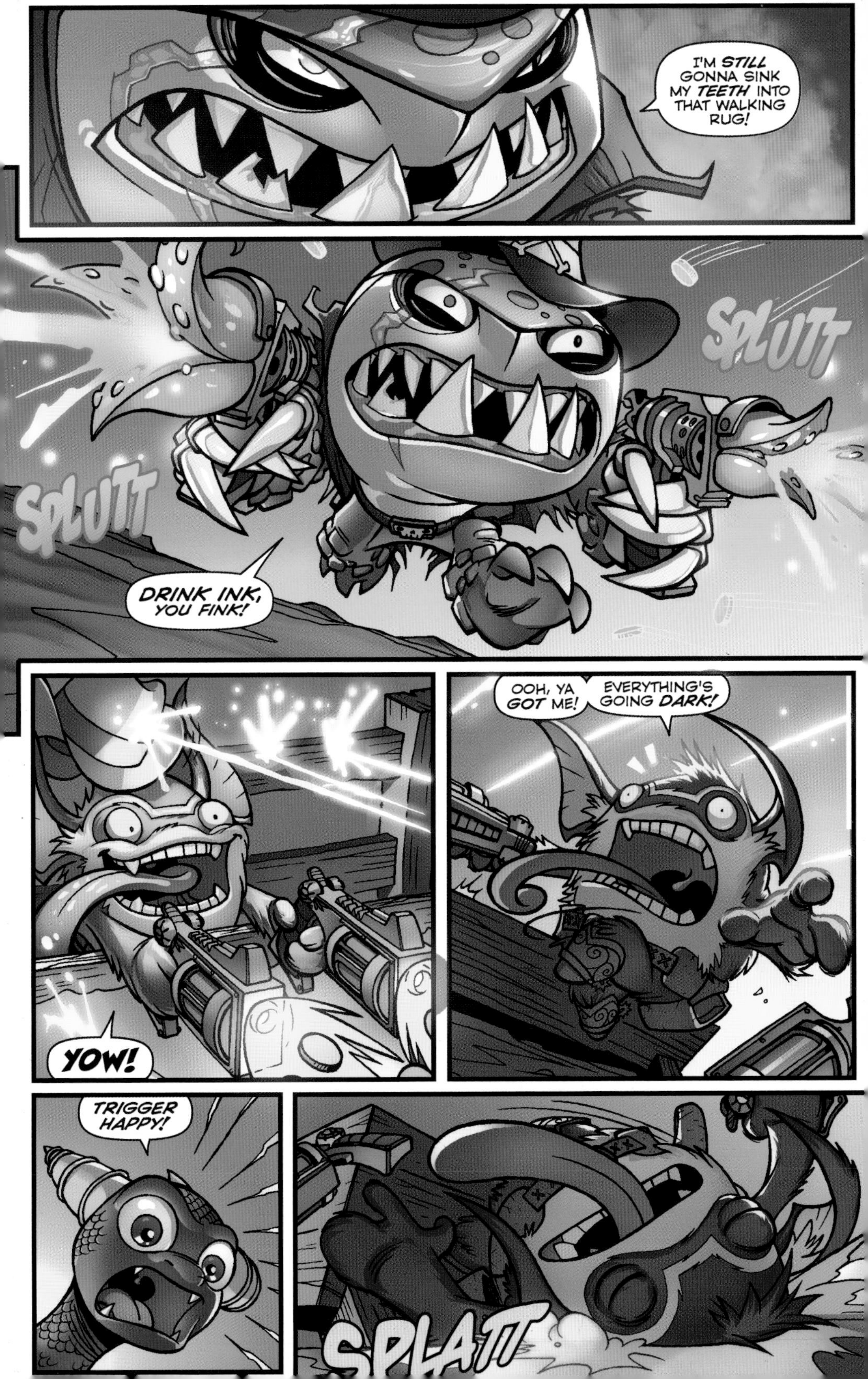
I'M STILL GONNA SINK MY TEETH INTO THAT WALKING RUG!
SPLUTT
SPLUTT
DRINK INK, YOU FINK!
YOW!
OOH, YA GOT ME!
EVERYTHING'S GOING DARK!
TRIGGER HAPPY!
SPLATT

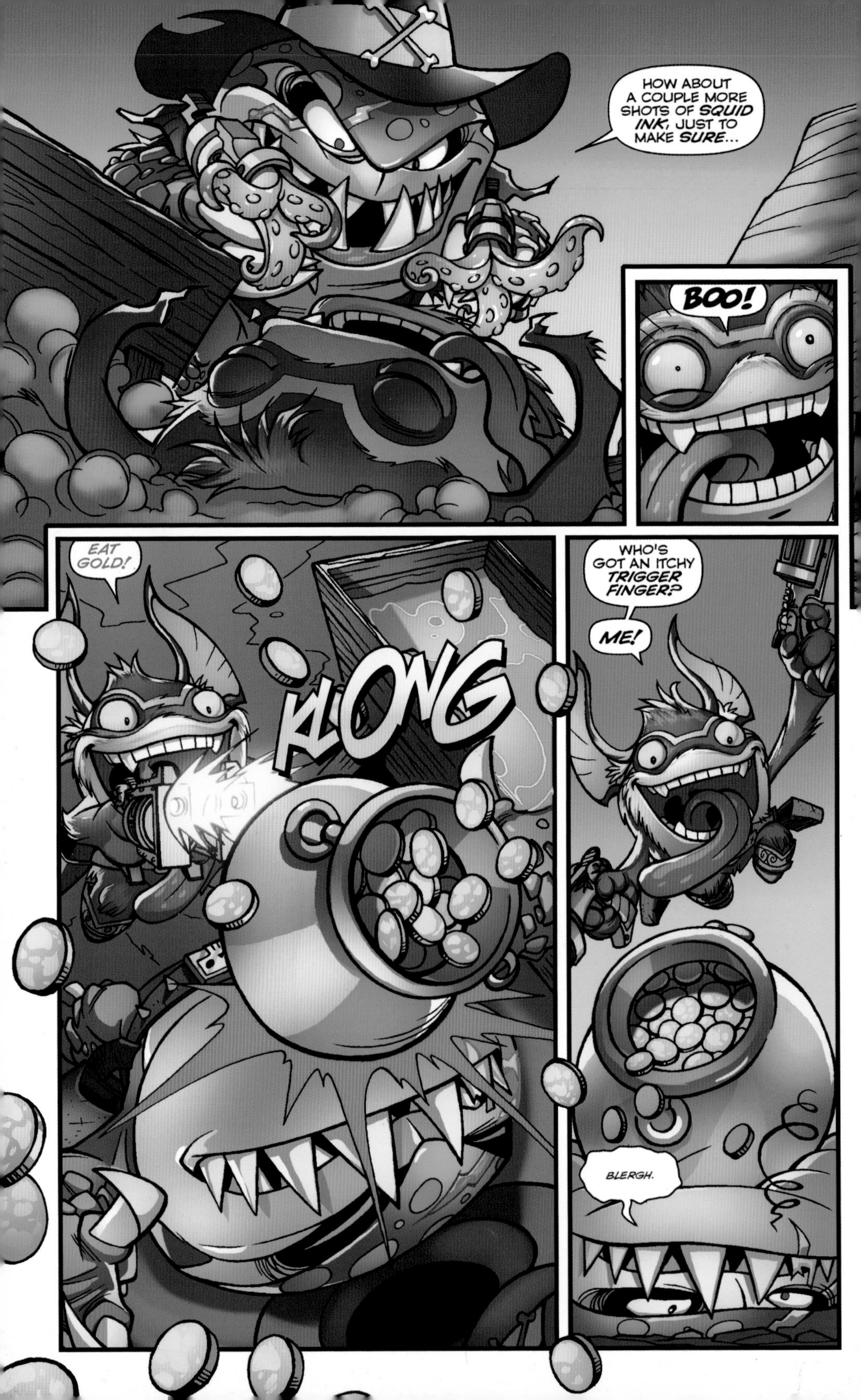
HOW ABOUT A COUPLE MORE SHOTS OF SQUID INK, JUST TO MAKE SURE...
BOO!
EAT GOLD!
KLONG
WHO'S GOT AN ITCHY TRIGGER FINGER?
ME!
BLERGH.

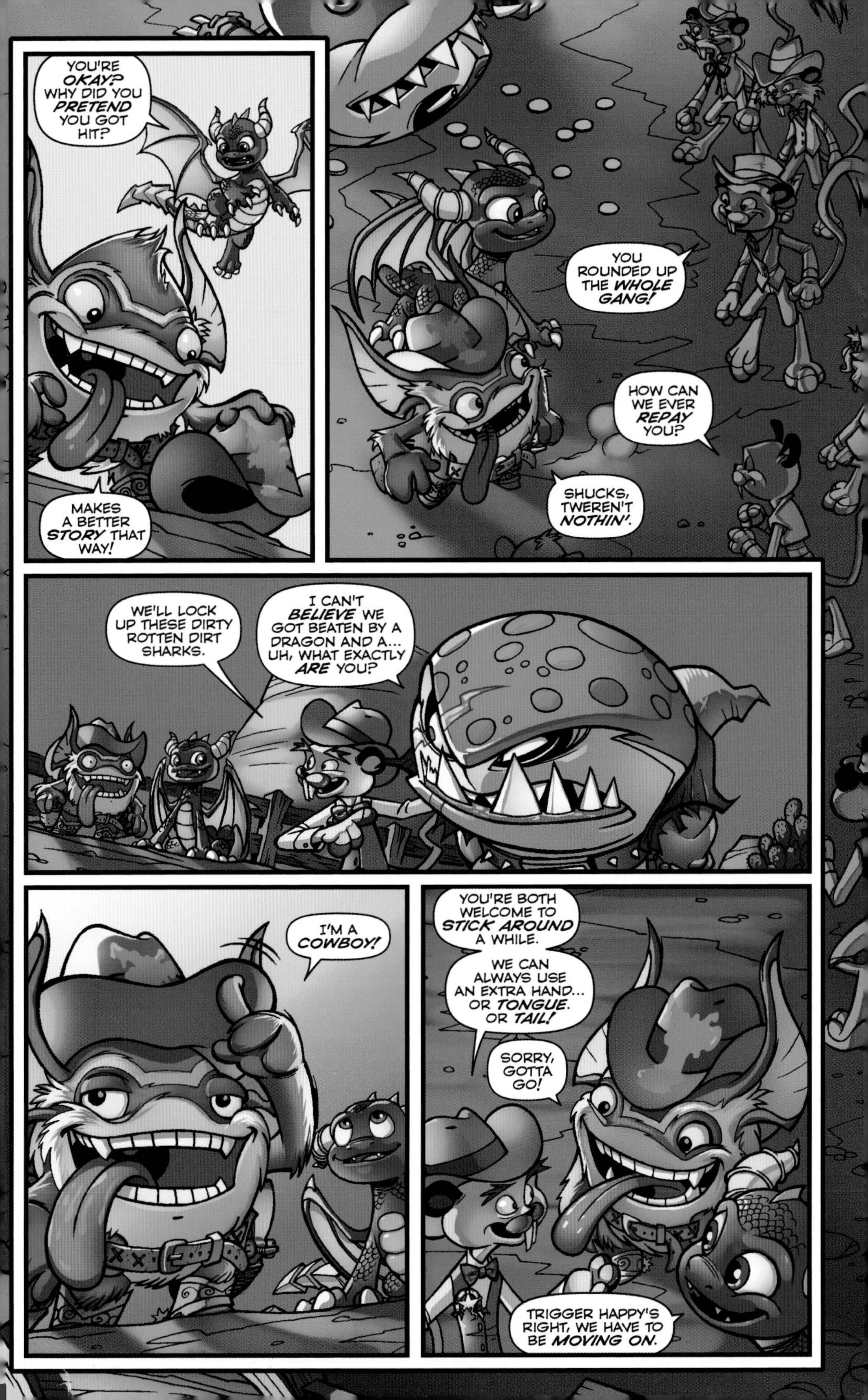
YOU'RE OKAY? WHY DID YOU PRETEND YOU GOT HIT?
MAKES A BETTER STORY THAT WAY!
YOU ROUNDED UP THE WHOLE GANG!
HOW CAN WE EVER REPAY YOU?
SHUCKS, TWEREN'T NOTHIN'.
WE'LL LOCK UP THESE DIRTY ROTTEN DIRT SHARKS.
I CAN'T BELIEVE WE GOT BEATEN BY A DRAGON AND A... UH, WHAT EXACTLY ARE YOU?
I'M A COWBOY!
YOU'RE BOTH WELCOME TO STICK AROUND A WHILE.
WE CAN ALWAYS USE AN EXTRA HAND... OR TONGUE. OR TAIL!
SORRY, GOTTA GO!
TRIGGER HAPPY'S RIGHT, WE HAVE TO BE MOVING ON.

SO WHERE TO NEXT...UH, PARDNER?
WE'RE RIDING OFF INTO THE SUNSET.
NO, I MEAN AFTER THAT.
MAYBE THE CLOUDBREAK ISLANDS?
DARK WATER COVE?
LEVIATHAN LAGOON?
NOPE.
NOPE.
AND NOPE.
WELL, I GUESS IT DOESN'T MATTER WHERE WE GO, AS LONG AS YOU DON'T HAVE ANY MORE CRAZY ADVENTURE SCHEMES.
CRAZY ADVENTURE SCHEMES? ME?
YOU MUST HAVE ME CONFUSED WITH SOME OTHER SKYLANDER.
SO... YOU EVER WANT TO BE A PIRATE?
END

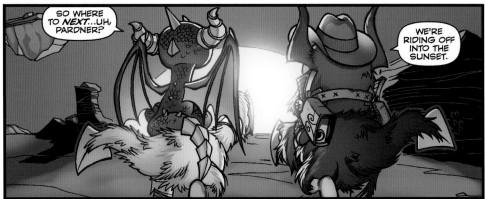

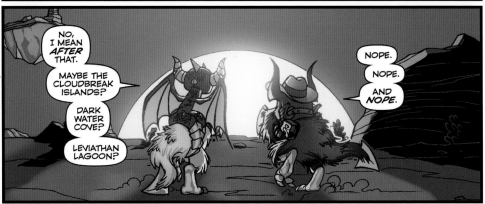

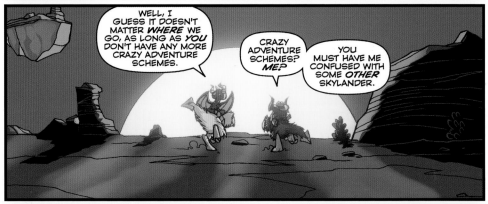

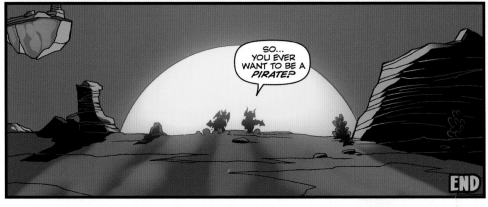

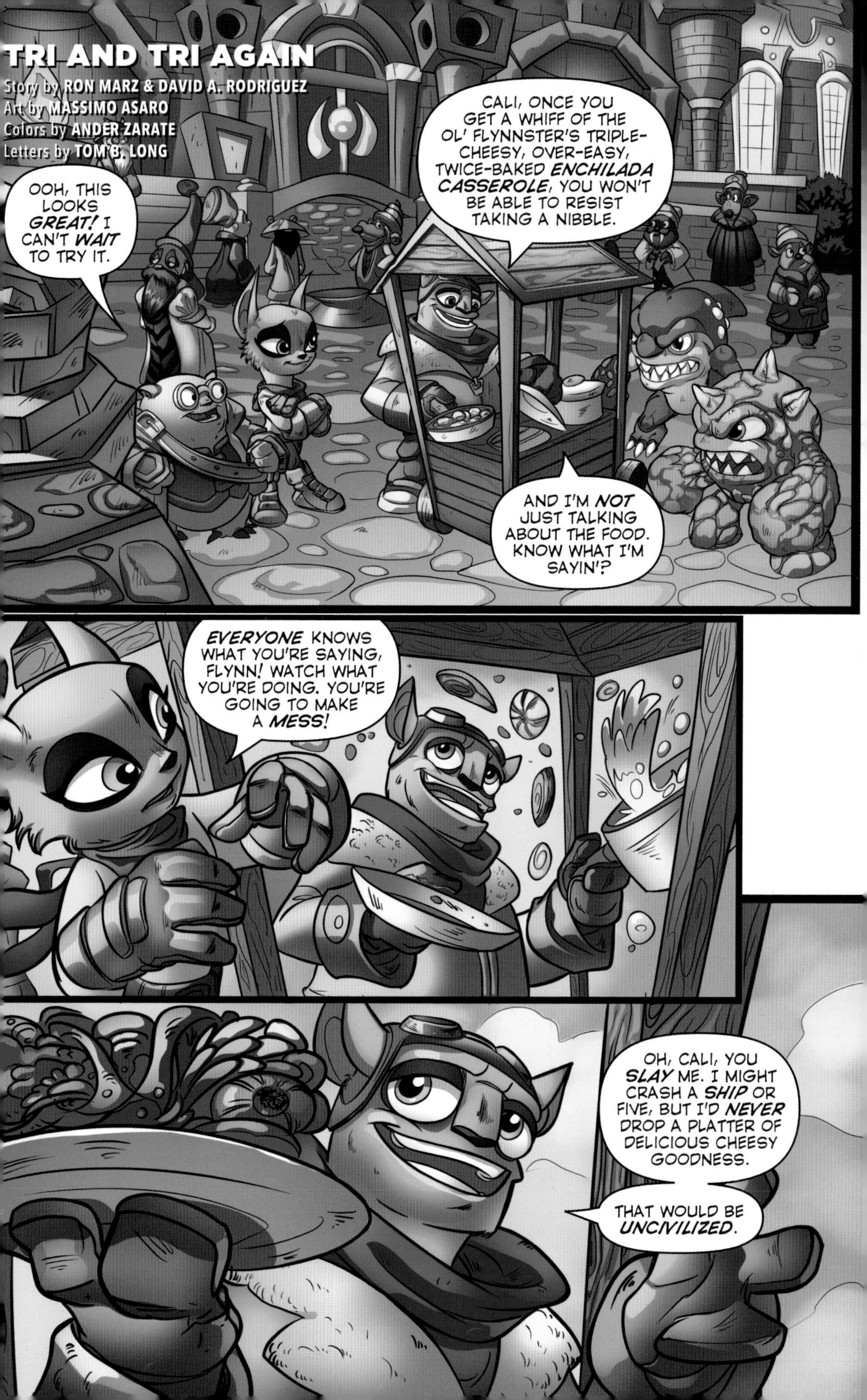
TRI AND TRI AGAIN
Story by RON MARZ & DAVID A. RODRIGUEZ
Art by MASSIMO ASARO
Colors by ANDER ZARATE
Letters by TOM B. LONG
OOH, THIS LOOKS GREAT! I CAN'T WAIT TO TRY IT.
CALI, ONCE YOU GET A WHIFF OF THE OL' FLYNNSTER'S TRIPLE-CHEESY, OVER-EASY, TWICE-BAKED ENCHILADA CASSEROLE, YOU WON'T BE ABLE TO RESIST TAKING A NIBBLE.
AND I'M NOT JUST TALKING ABOUT THE FOOD. KNOW WHAT I'M SAYIN'?
EVERYONE KNOWS WHAT YOU'RE SAYING, FLYNN! WATCH WHAT YOU'RE DOING. YOU'RE GOING TO MAKE A MESS!
OH, CALI, YOU SLAY ME. I MIGHT CRASH A SHIP OR FIVE, BUT I'D NEVER DROP A PLATTER OF DELICIOUS CHEESY GOODNESS.
THAT WOULD BE UNCIVILIZED.

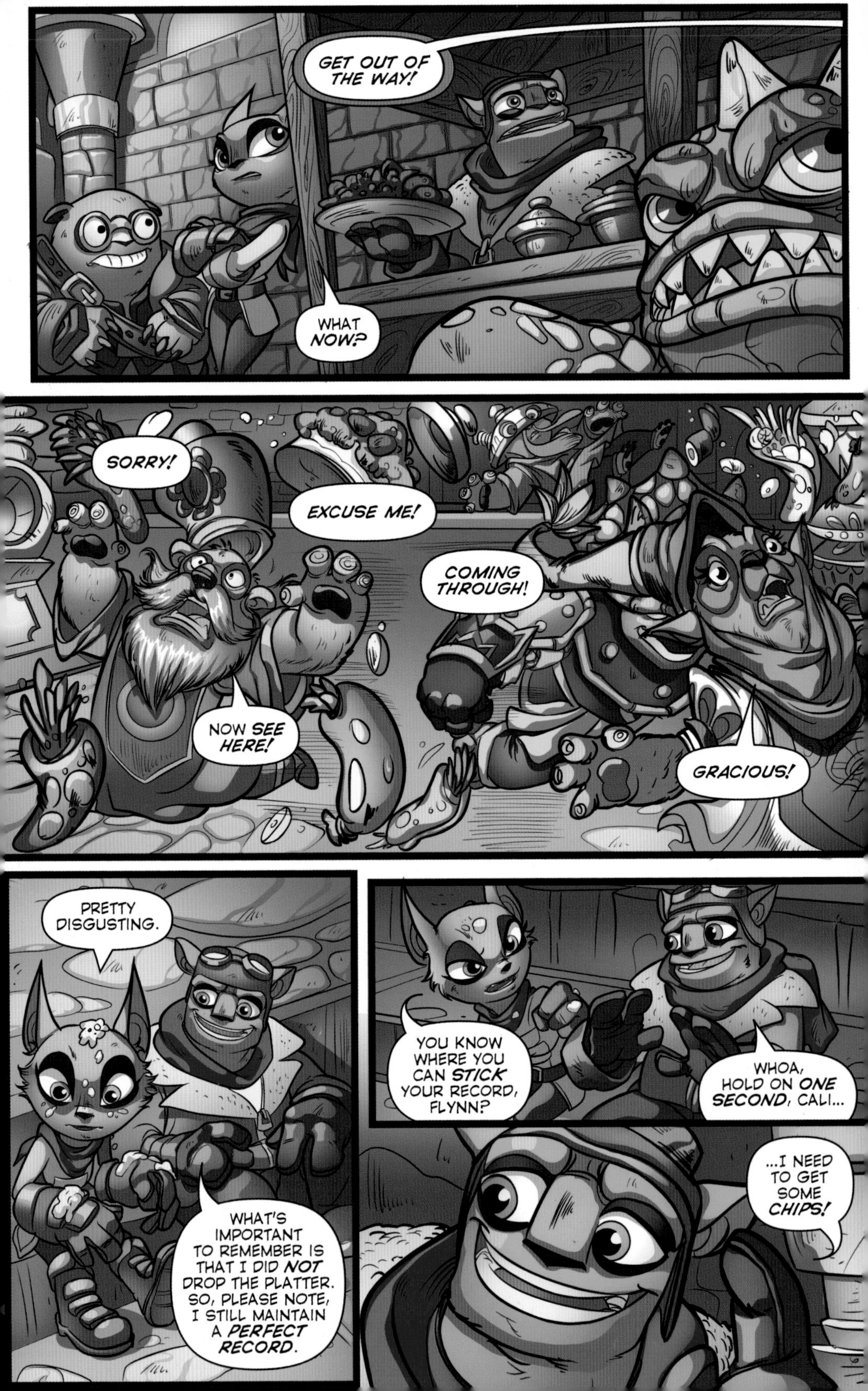
GET OUT OF THE WAY!
WHAT NOW?
SORRY!
EXCUSE ME!
COMING THROUGH!
NOW SEE HERE!
GRACIOUS!
PRETTY DISGUSTING.
WHAT'S IMPORTANT TO REMEMBER IS THAT I DID NOT DROP THE PLATTER. SO, PLEASE NOTE, I STILL MAINTAIN A PERFECT RECORD.
YOU KNOW WHERE YOU CAN STICK YOUR RECORD, FLYNN?
WHOA, HOLD ON ONE SECOND, CALI...
...I NEED TO GET SOME CHIPS!

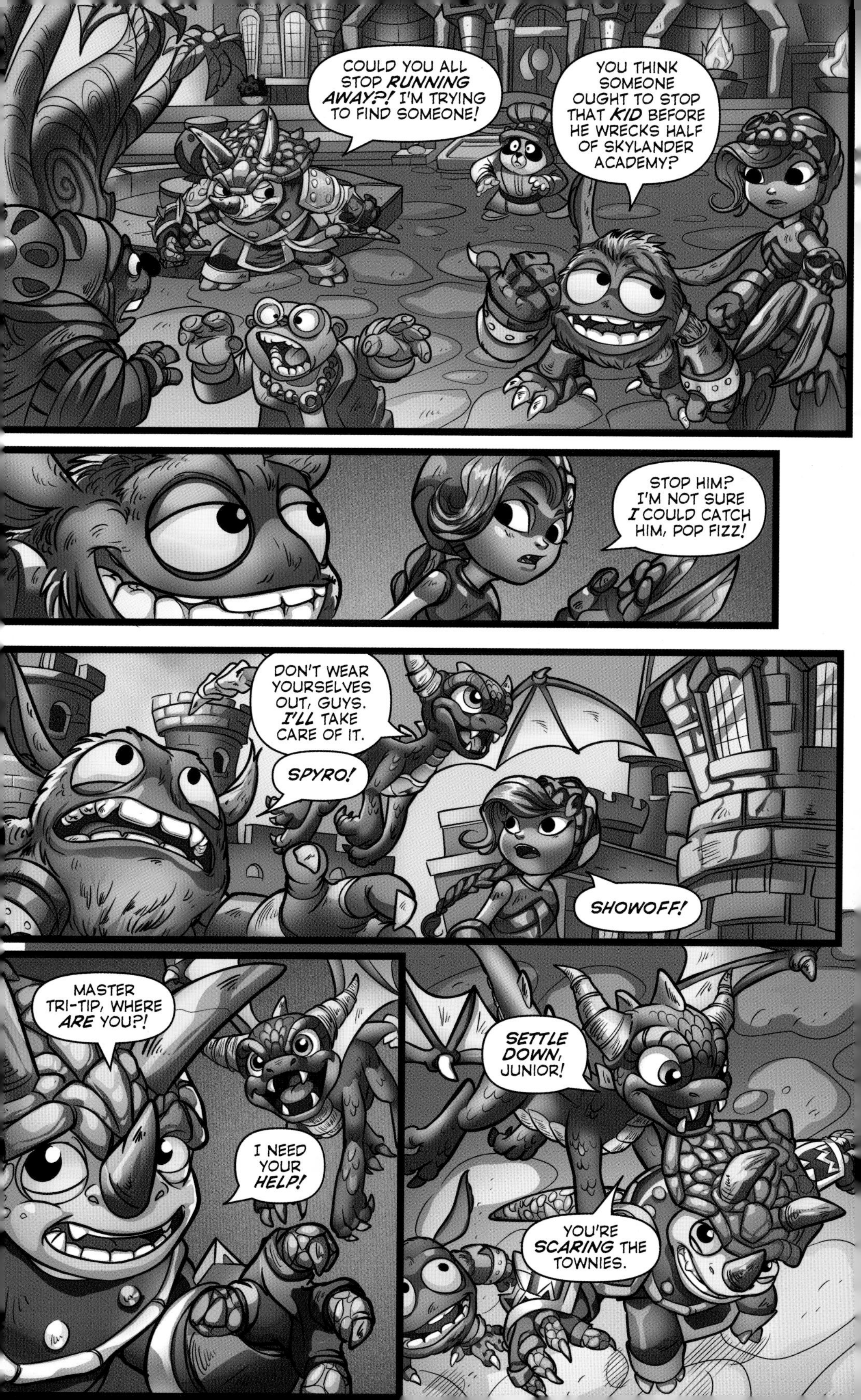
COULD YOU ALL STOP RUNNING AWAY?! I'M TRYING TO FIND SOMEONE!
YOU THINK SOMEONE OUGHT TO STOP THAT KID BEFORE HE WRECKS HALF OF SKYLANDER ACADEMY?
STOP HIM? I'M NOT SURE I COULD CATCH HIM, POP FIZZ!
DON'T WEAR YOURSELVES OUT, GUYS. I'LL TAKE CARE OF IT.
SPYRO!
SHOWOFF!
MASTER TRI-TIP, WHERE ARE YOU?!
I NEED YOUR HELP!
SETTLE DOWN, JUNIOR!
YOU'RE SCARING THE TOWNIES.

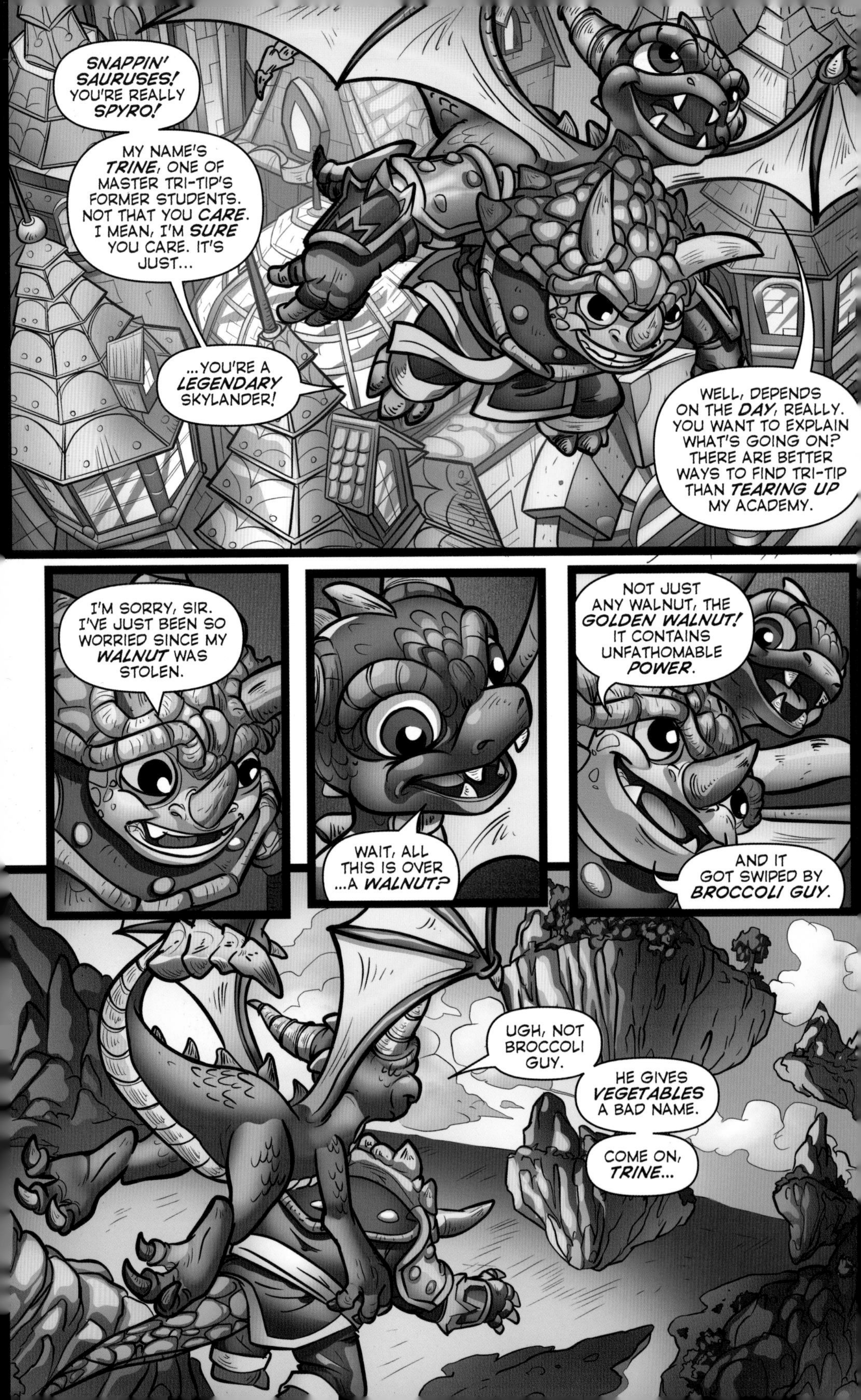
SNAPPIN' SAURUSES! YOU'RE REALLY SPYRO!
MY NAME'S TRINE, ONE OF MASTER TRI-TIP'S FORMER STUDENTS. NOT THAT YOU CARE. I MEAN, I'M SURE YOU CARE. IT'S JUST...
...YOU'RE A LEGENDARY SKYLANDER!
WELL, DEPENDS ON THE DAY, REALLY. YOU WANT TO EXPLAIN WHAT'S GOING ON? THERE ARE BETTER WAYS TO FIND TRI-TIP THAN TEARING UP MY ACADEMY.
I'M SORRY, SIR. I'VE JUST BEEN SO WORRIED SINCE MY WALNUT WAS STOLEN.
WAIT, ALL THIS IS OVER ...A WALNUT?
NOT JUST ANY WALNUT, THE GOLDEN WALNUT! IT CONTAINS UNFATHOMABLE POWER.
AND IT GOT SWIPED BY BROCCOLI GUY.
UGH, NOT BROCCOLI GUY.
HE GIVES VEGETABLES A BAD NAME.
COME ON, TRINE...

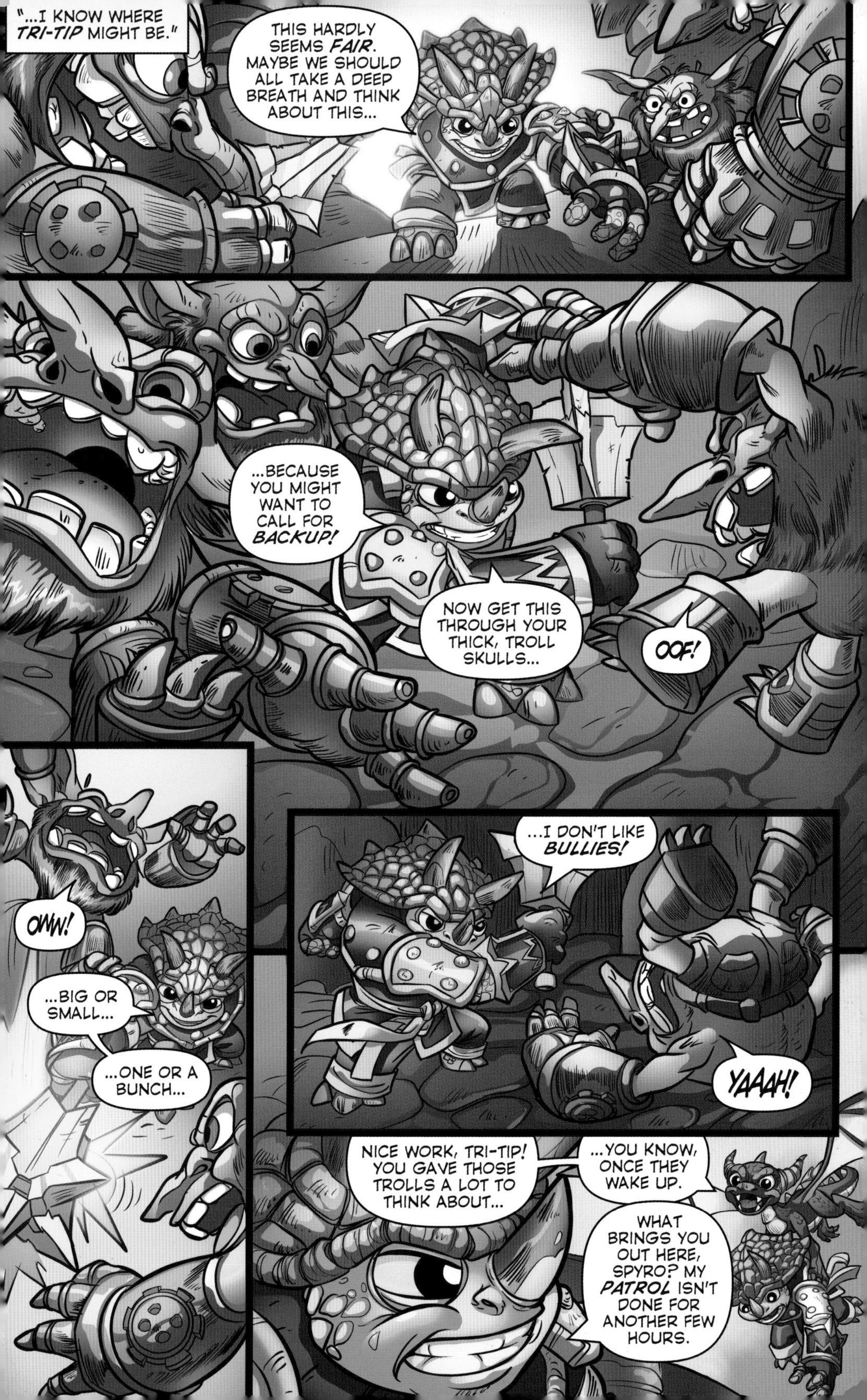
"...I KNOW WHERE *TRI-TIP* MIGHT BE."
THIS HARDLY SEEMS *FAIR*. MAYBE WE SHOULD ALL TAKE A DEEP BREATH AND THINK ABOUT THIS...
...BECAUSE YOU MIGHT WANT TO CALL FOR *BACKUP!*
NOW GET THIS THROUGH YOUR THICK, TROLL SKULLS...
OOF!
OWW!
...BIG OR SMALL...
...ONE OR A BUNCH...
...I DON'T LIKE *BULLIES!*
YAAAH!
NICE WORK, TRI-TIP! YOU GAVE THOSE TROLLS A LOT TO THINK ABOUT...
...YOU KNOW, ONCE THEY WAKE UP.
WHAT BRINGS YOU OUT HERE, SPYRO? MY *PATROL* ISN'T DONE FOR ANOTHER FEW HOURS.

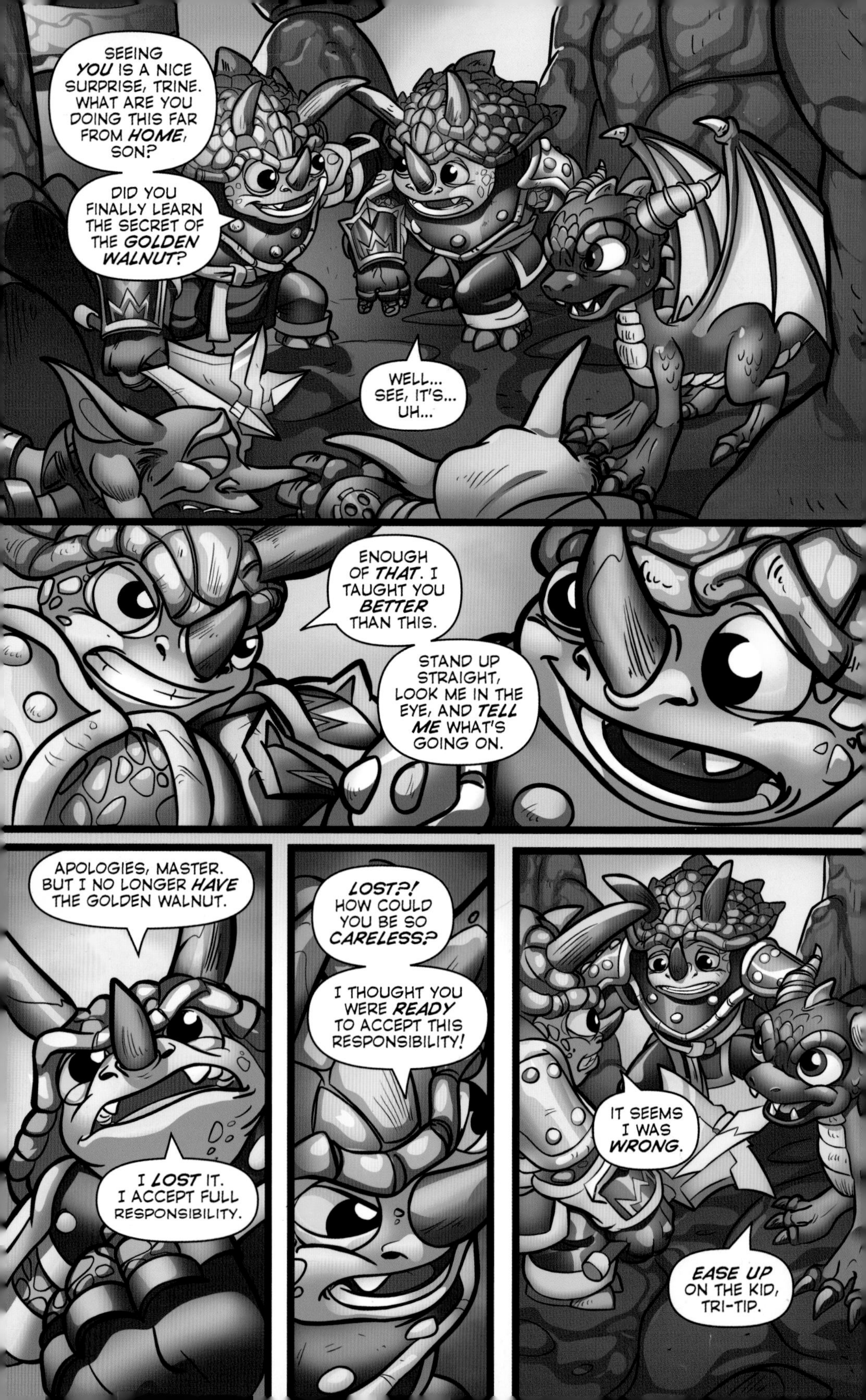

SEEING YOU IS A NICE SURPRISE, TRINE. WHAT ARE YOU DOING THIS FAR FROM HOME, SON?
DID YOU FINALLY LEARN THE SECRET OF THE GOLDEN WALNUT?
WELL... SEE, IT'S... UH...
ENOUGH OF THAT. I TAUGHT YOU BETTER THAN THIS.
STAND UP STRAIGHT, LOOK ME IN THE EYE, AND TELL ME WHAT'S GOING ON.
APOLOGIES, MASTER. BUT I NO LONGER HAVE THE GOLDEN WALNUT.
I LOST IT. I ACCEPT FULL RESPONSIBILITY.
LOST?! HOW COULD YOU BE SO CARELESS?
I THOUGHT YOU WERE READY TO ACCEPT THIS RESPONSIBILITY!
IT SEEMS I WAS WRONG.
EASE UP ON THE KID, TRI-TIP.

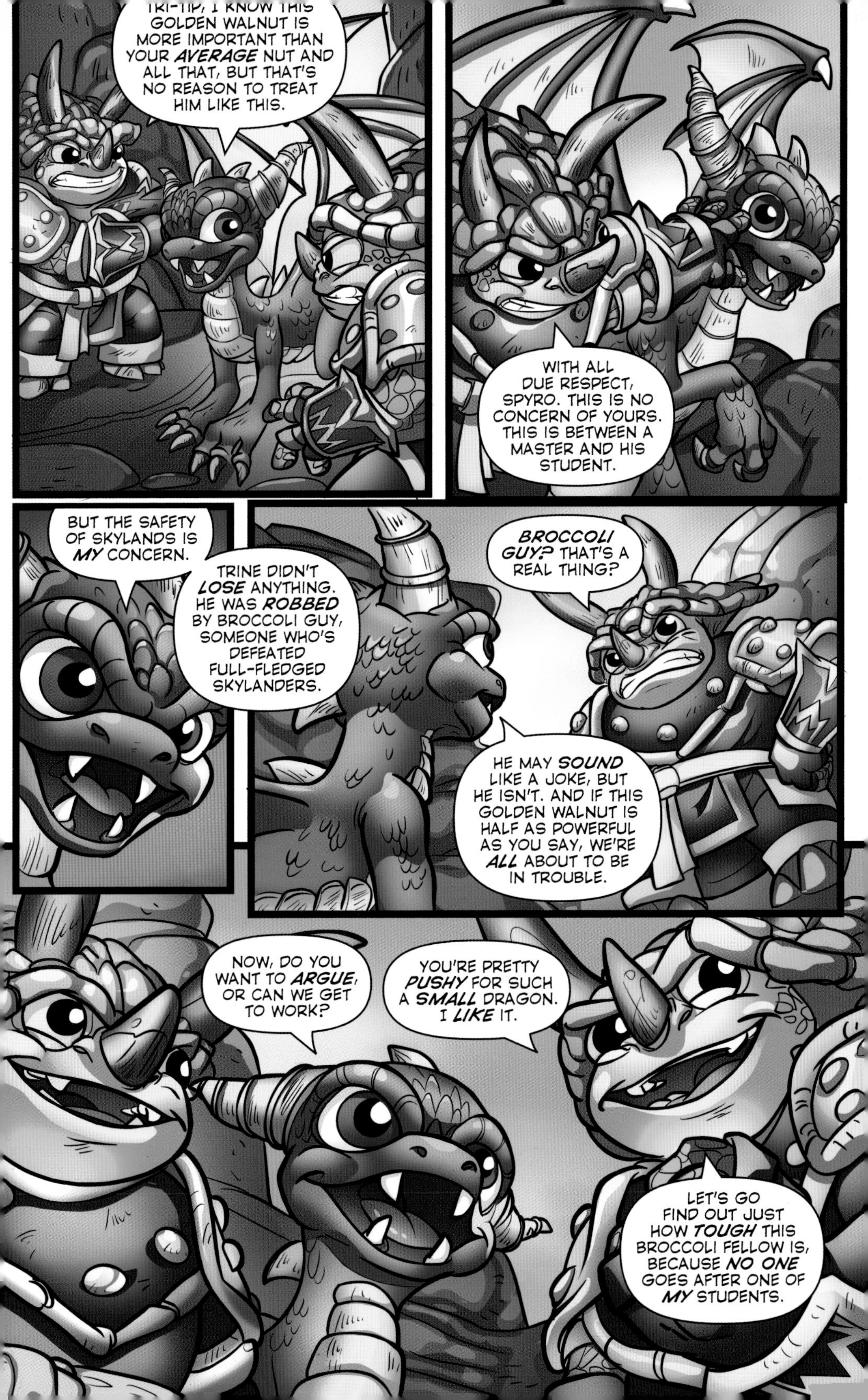
TRI-TIP, I KNOW THIS GOLDEN WALNUT IS MORE IMPORTANT THAN YOUR *AVERAGE* NUT AND ALL THAT, BUT THAT'S NO REASON TO TREAT HIM LIKE THIS.
WITH ALL DUE RESPECT, SPYRO. THIS IS NO CONCERN OF YOURS. THIS IS BETWEEN A MASTER AND HIS STUDENT.
BUT THE SAFETY OF SKYLANDS IS *MY* CONCERN.
TRINE DIDN'T *LOSE* ANYTHING. HE WAS *ROBBED* BY BROCCOLI GUY, SOMEONE WHO'S DEFEATED FULL-FLEDGED SKYLANDERS.
*BROCCOLI GUY?* THAT'S A REAL THING?
HE MAY *SOUND* LIKE A JOKE, BUT HE ISN'T. AND IF THIS GOLDEN WALNUT IS HALF AS POWERFUL AS YOU SAY, WE'RE *ALL* ABOUT TO BE IN TROUBLE.
NOW, DO YOU WANT TO *ARGUE*, OR CAN WE GET TO WORK?
YOU'RE PRETTY *PUSHY* FOR SUCH A *SMALL* DRAGON. I *LIKE* IT.
LET'S GO FIND OUT JUST HOW *TOUGH* THIS BROCCOLI FELLOW IS, BECAUSE *NO ONE* GOES AFTER ONE OF *MY* STUDENTS.

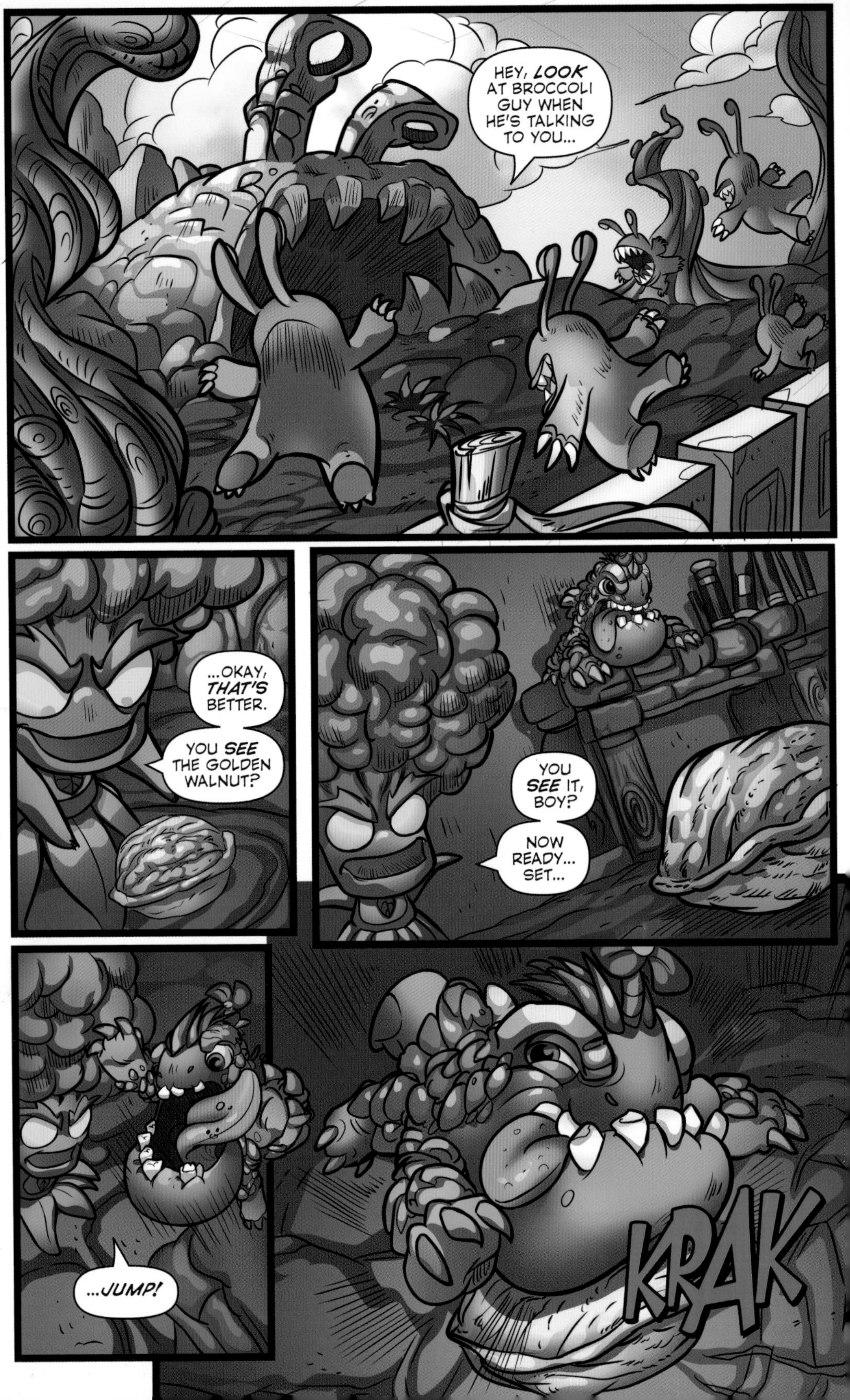

HEY, LOOK AT BROCCOLI GUY WHEN HE'S TALKING TO YOU...
...OKAY, THAT'S BETTER.
YOU SEE THE GOLDEN WALNUT?
YOU SEE IT, BOY?
NOW READY... SET...
...JUMP!
KRAK

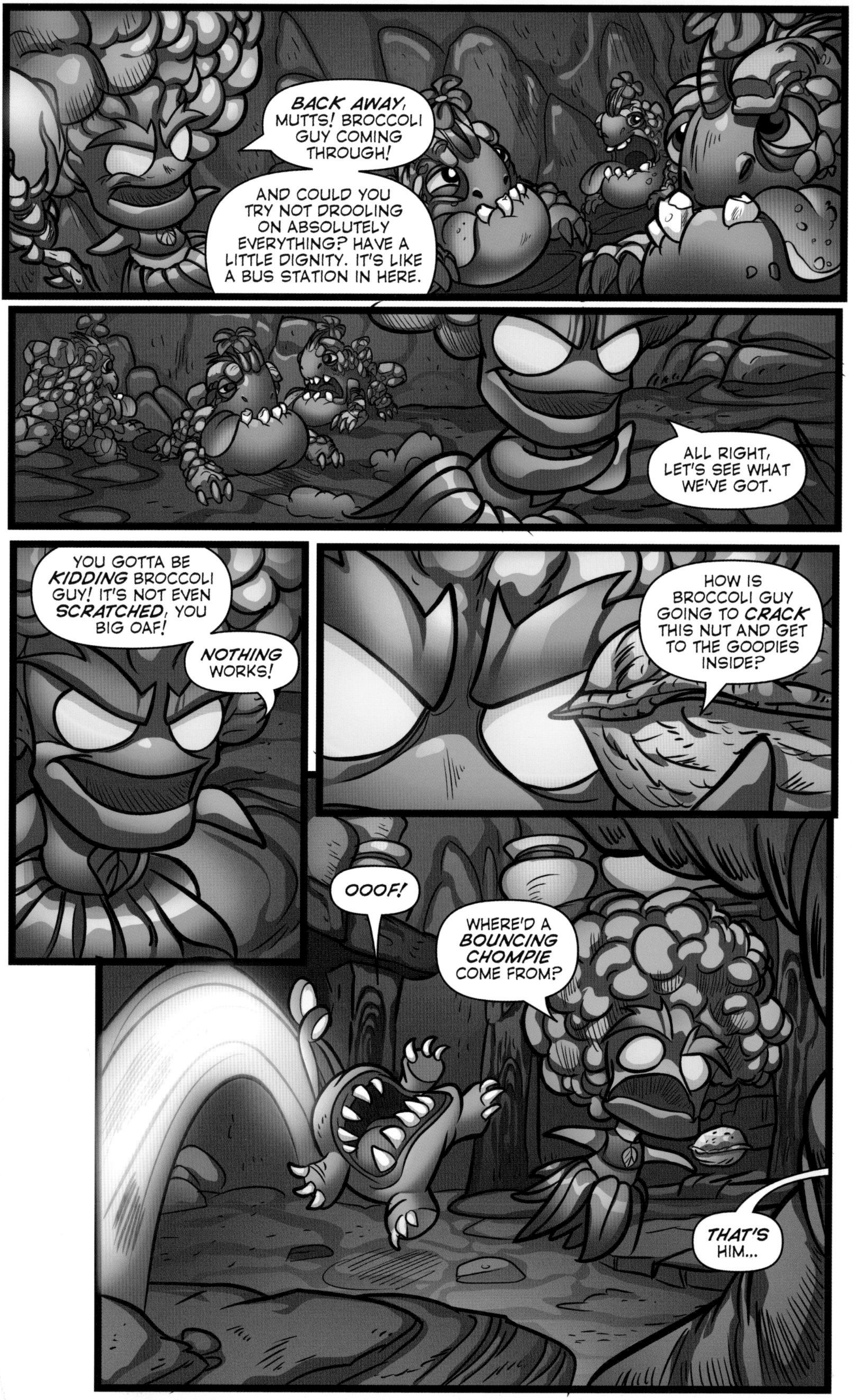
BACK AWAY, MUTTS! BROCCOLI GUY COMING THROUGH!
AND COULD YOU TRY NOT DROOLING ON ABSOLUTELY EVERYTHING? HAVE A LITTLE DIGNITY. IT'S LIKE A BUS STATION IN HERE.
ALL RIGHT, LET'S SEE WHAT WE'VE GOT.
YOU GOTTA BE KIDDING BROCCOLI GUY! IT'S NOT EVEN SCRATCHED, YOU BIG OAF!
NOTHING WORKS!
HOW IS BROCCOLI GUY GOING TO CRACK THIS NUT AND GET TO THE GOODIES INSIDE?
OOOF!
WHERE'D A BOUNCING CHOMPIE COME FROM?
THAT'S HIM...

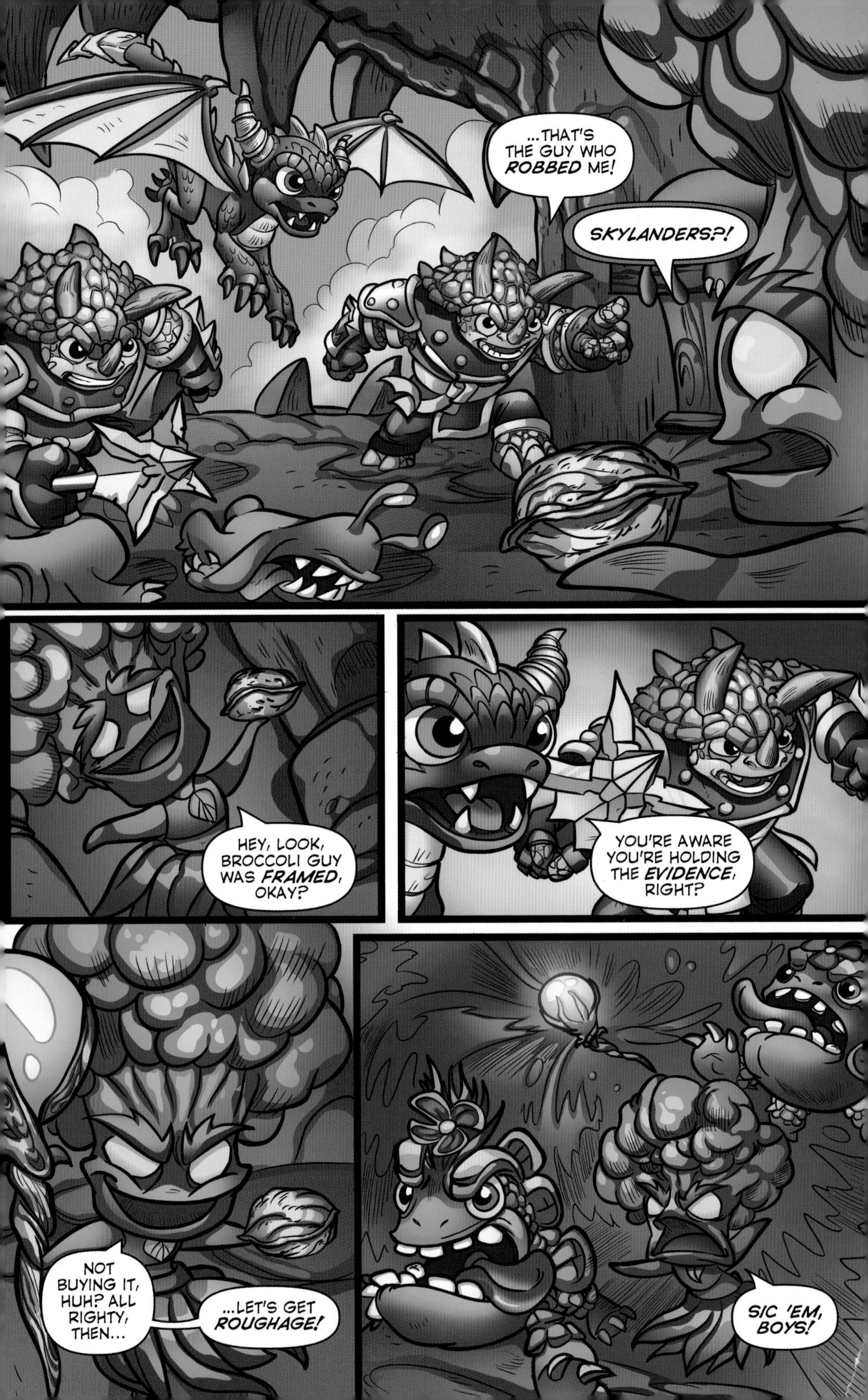

...THAT'S THE GUY WHO *ROBBED* ME!
*SKYLANDERS?!*
HEY, LOOK, BROCCOLI GUY WAS *FRAMED*, OKAY?
YOU'RE AWARE YOU'RE HOLDING THE *EVIDENCE*, RIGHT?
NOT BUYING IT, HUH? ALL RIGHTY, THEN...
...LET'S GET *ROUGHAGE!*
*SIC 'EM, BOYS!*

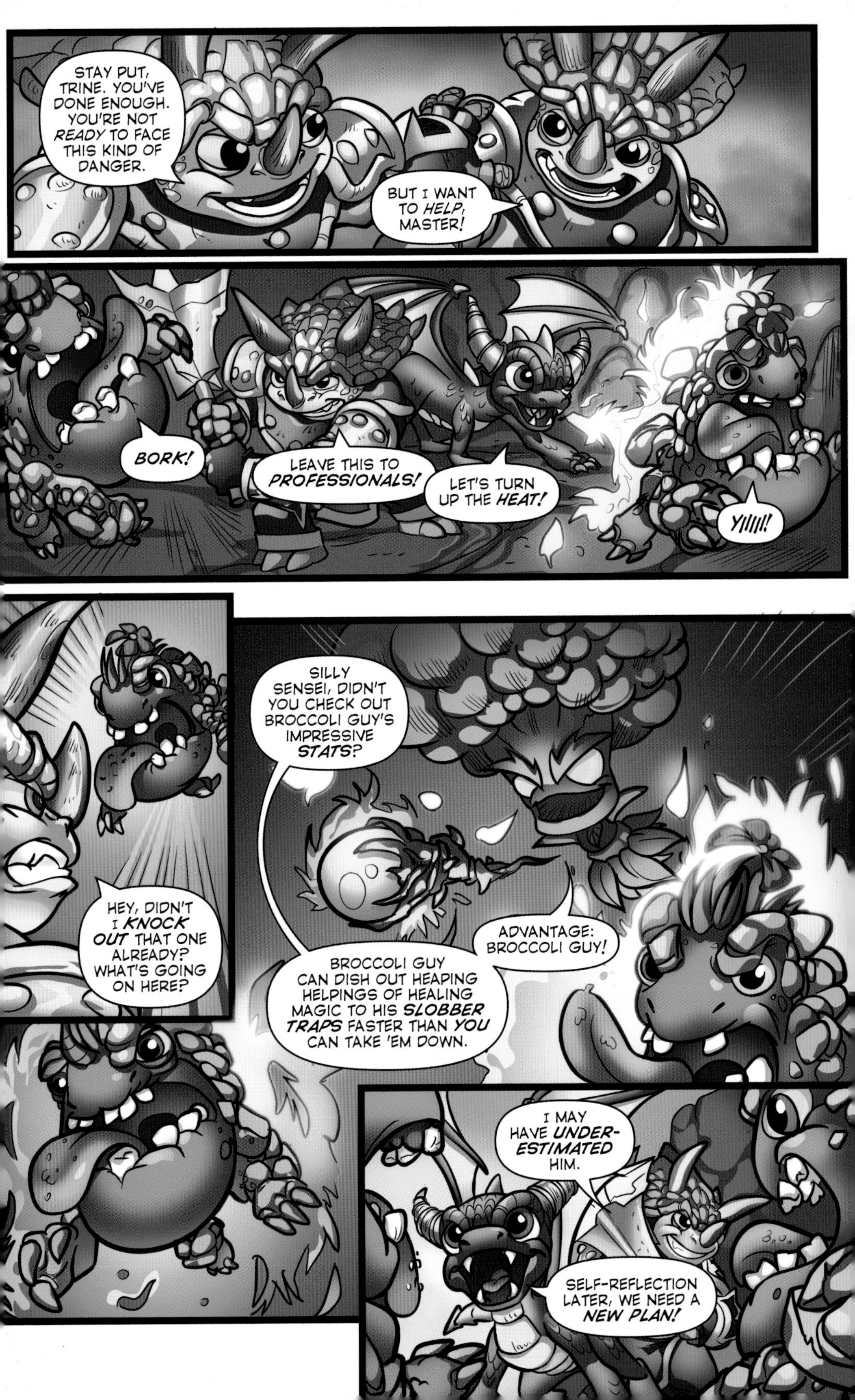
STAY PUT, TRINE. YOU'VE DONE ENOUGH. YOU'RE NOT READY TO FACE THIS KIND OF DANGER.
BUT I WANT TO HELP, MASTER!
BORK!
LEAVE THIS TO PROFESSIONALS!
LET'S TURN UP THE HEAT!
YIIII!
HEY, DIDN'T I KNOCK OUT THAT ONE ALREADY? WHAT'S GOING ON HERE?
SILLY SENSEI, DIDN'T YOU CHECK OUT BROCCOLI GUY'S IMPRESSIVE STATS?
ADVANTAGE: BROCCOLI GUY!
BROCCOLI GUY CAN DISH OUT HEAPING HELPINGS OF HEALING MAGIC TO HIS SLOBBER TRAPS FASTER THAN YOU CAN TAKE 'EM DOWN.
I MAY HAVE UNDER-ESTIMATED HIM.
SELF-REFLECTION LATER, WE NEED A NEW PLAN!

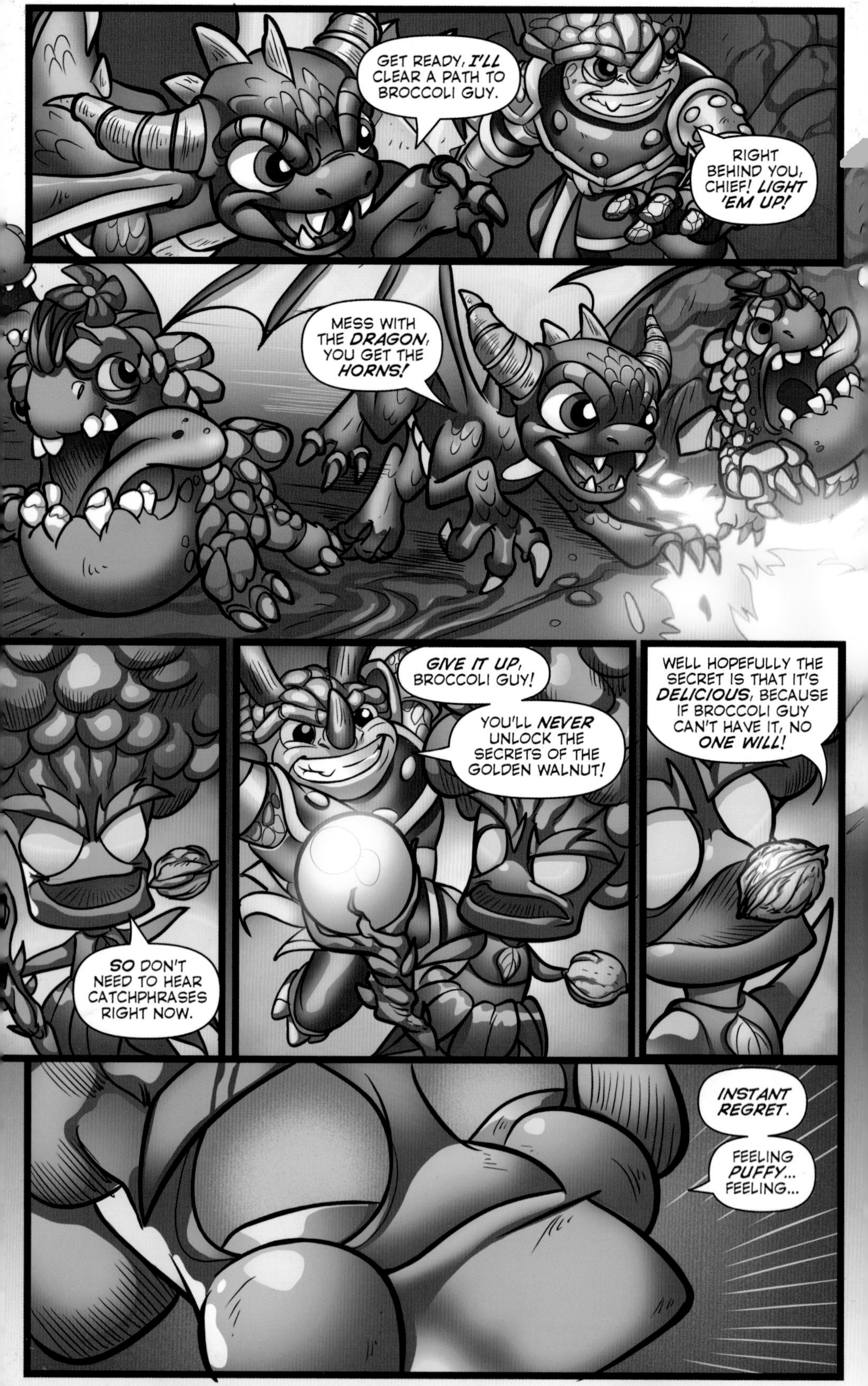
GET READY, *I'LL* CLEAR A PATH TO BROCCOLI GUY.
RIGHT BEHIND YOU, CHIEF! *LIGHT 'EM UP!*
MESS WITH THE *DRAGON*, YOU GET THE *HORNS!*
*SO* DON'T NEED TO HEAR CATCHPHRASES RIGHT NOW.
*GIVE IT UP*, BROCCOLI GUY!
YOU'LL *NEVER* UNLOCK THE SECRETS OF THE GOLDEN WALNUT!
WELL HOPEFULLY THE SECRET IS THAT IT'S *DELICIOUS*, BECAUSE IF BROCCOLI GUY CAN'T HAVE IT, NO *ONE WILL!*
*INSTANT REGRET*.
FEELING *PUFFY*... FEELING...

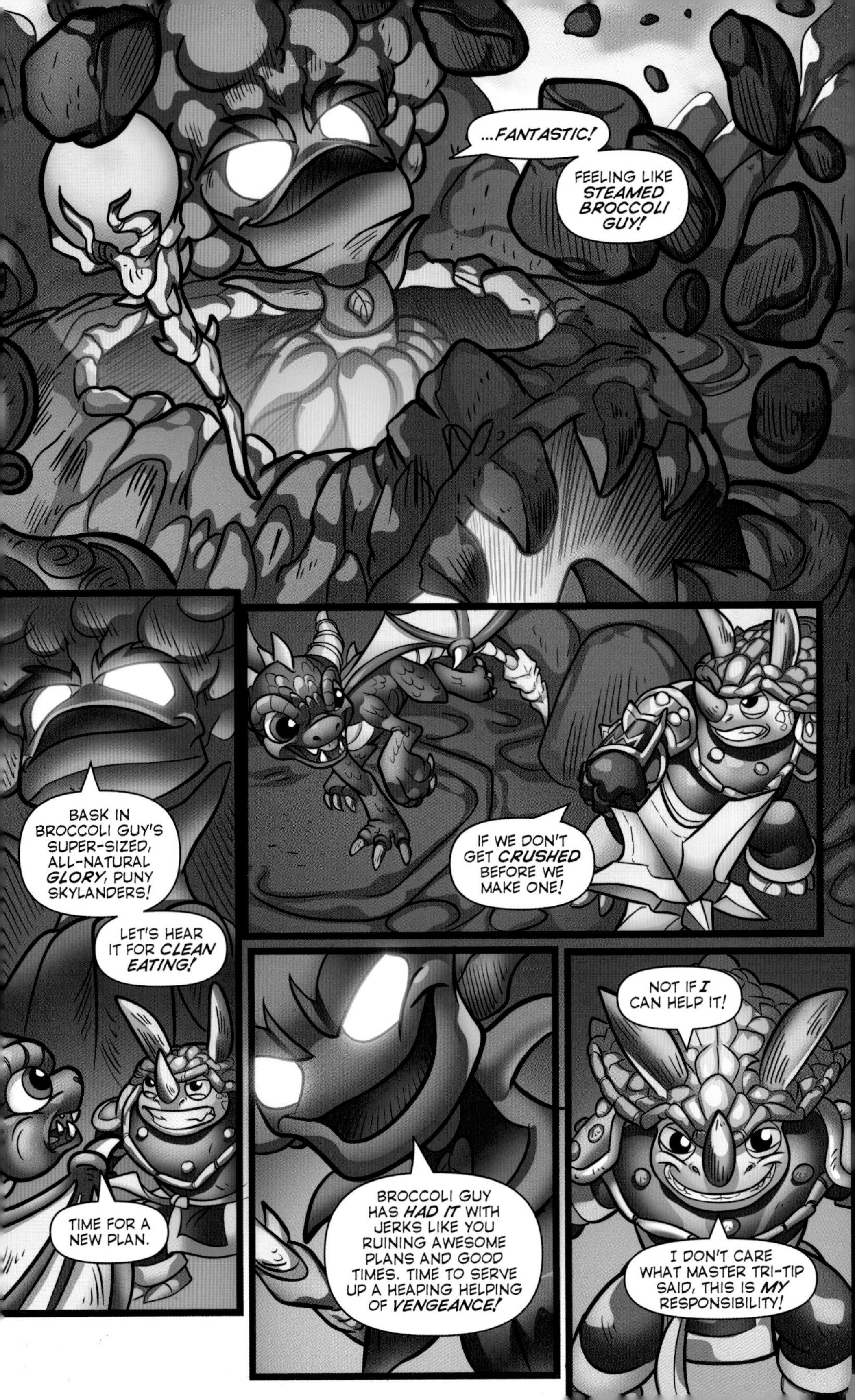
...FANTASTIC!
FEELING LIKE STEAMED BROCCOLI GUY!
BASK IN BROCCOLI GUY'S SUPER-SIZED, ALL-NATURAL GLORY, PUNY SKYLANDERS!
LET'S HEAR IT FOR CLEAN EATING!
IF WE DON'T GET CRUSHED BEFORE WE MAKE ONE!
TIME FOR A NEW PLAN.
BROCCOLI GUY HAS HAD IT WITH JERKS LIKE YOU RUINING AWESOME PLANS AND GOOD TIMES. TIME TO SERVE UP A HEAPING HELPING OF VENGEANCE!
NOT IF I CAN HELP IT!
I DON'T CARE WHAT MASTER TRI-TIP SAID, THIS IS MY RESPONSIBILITY!

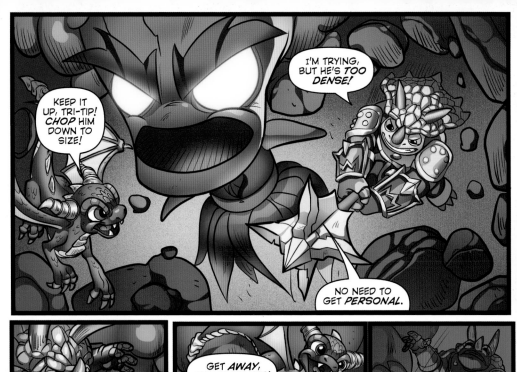

KEEP IT UP, TRI-TIP! *CHOP* HIM DOWN TO SIZE!

I'M TRYING, BUT HE'S *TOO DENSE!*

NO NEED TO GET *PERSONAL.*

BESIDES, BROCCOLI GUY IS NOT DENSE, HE'S *FORTIFIED!*

GET *AWAY,* YOU NUISANCE!

WHFF!

HANG ON, MASTER!

THE GREAT TRI-TIP, ABOUT TO BE *SQUISHED* BY A GIANT STALK OF PRODUCE!

LET HIM *GO!*

AHRRG!

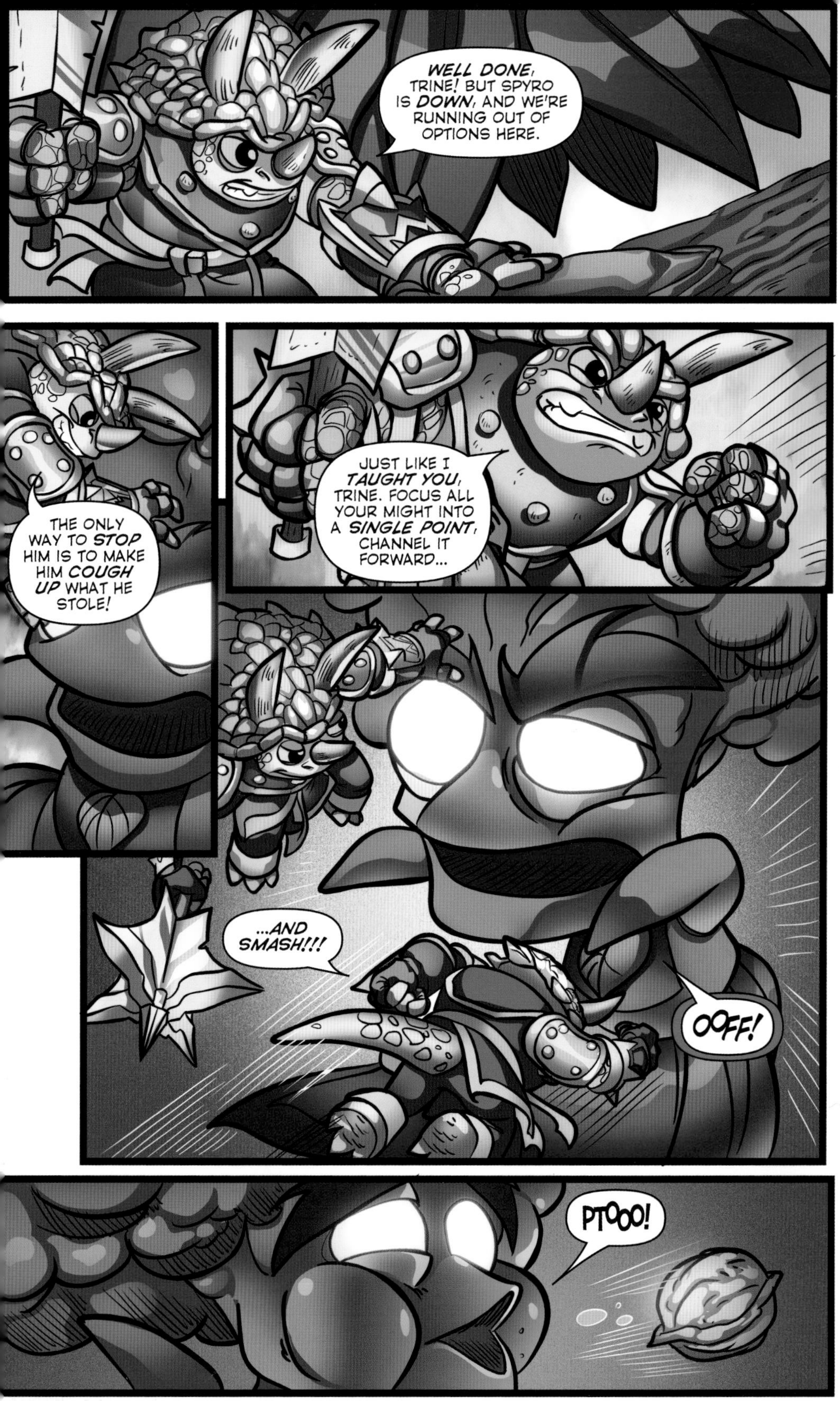
WELL DONE, TRINE! BUT SPYRO IS DOWN, AND WE'RE RUNNING OUT OF OPTIONS HERE.
THE ONLY WAY TO STOP HIM IS TO MAKE HIM COUGH UP WHAT HE STOLE!
JUST LIKE I TAUGHT YOU, TRINE. FOCUS ALL YOUR MIGHT INTO A SINGLE POINT, CHANNEL IT FORWARD...
...AND SMASH!!!
OOFF!
PTOOO!

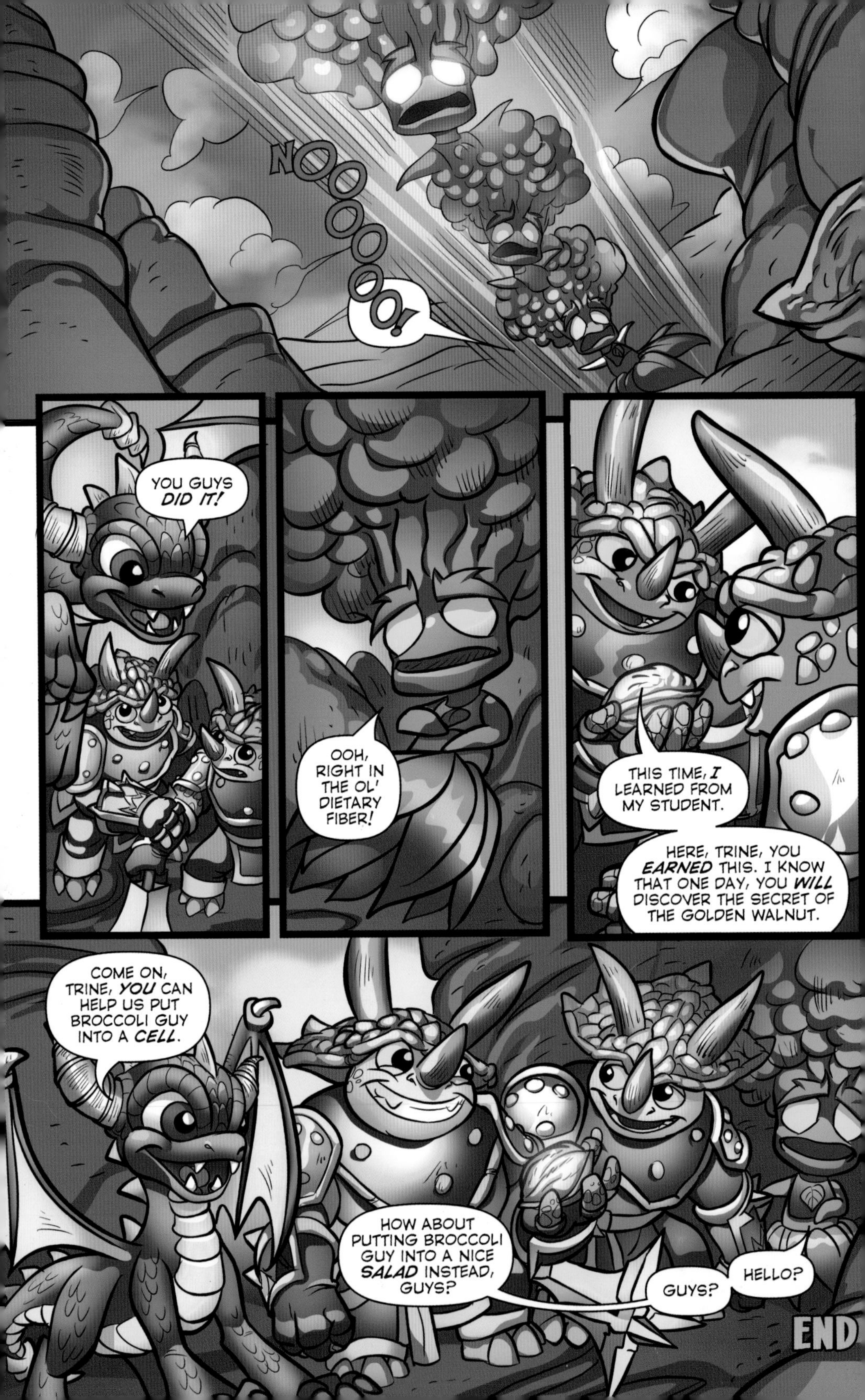
NOOOOOOOO!
YOU GUYS DID IT!
OOH, RIGHT IN THE OL' DIETARY FIBER!
THIS TIME, I LEARNED FROM MY STUDENT.
HERE, TRINE, YOU EARNED THIS. I KNOW THAT ONE DAY, YOU WILL DISCOVER THE SECRET OF THE GOLDEN WALNUT.
COME ON, TRINE, YOU CAN HELP US PUT BROCCOLI GUY INTO A CELL.
HOW ABOUT PUTTING BROCCOLI GUY INTO A NICE SALAD INSTEAD, GUYS?
GUYS?
HELLO?
END

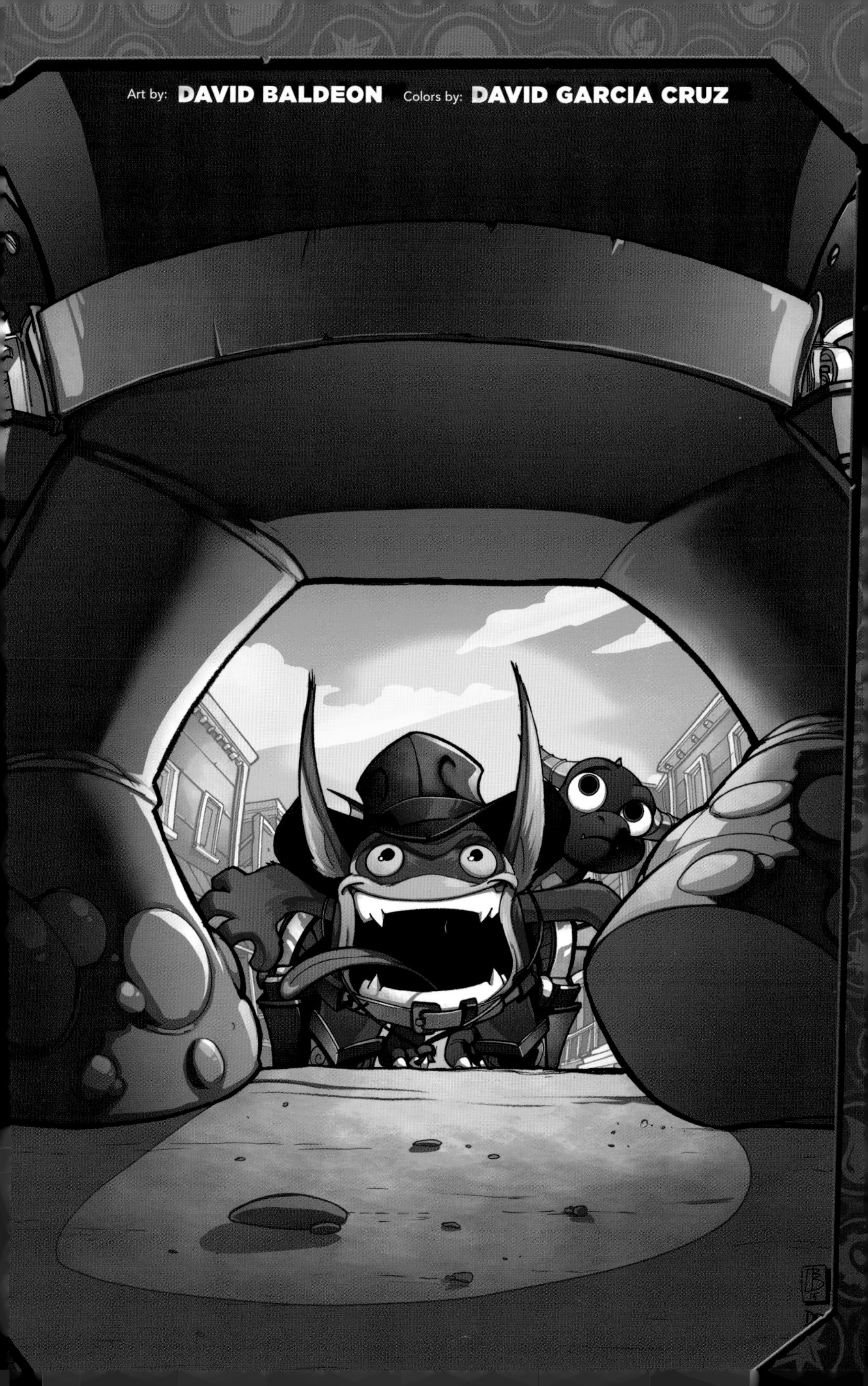
Art by: DAVID BALDEON Colors by: DAVID GARCIA CRUZ

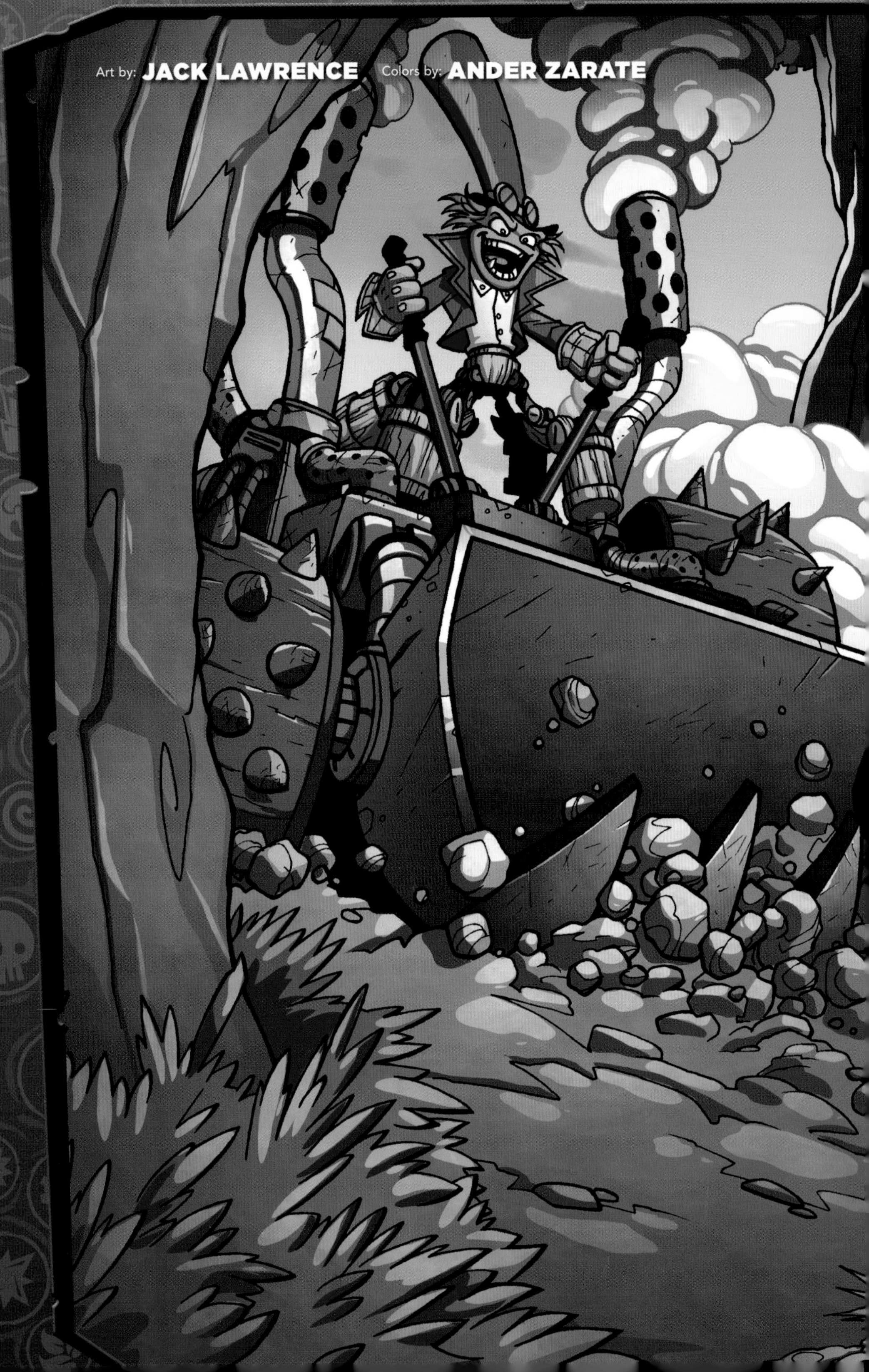
Art by: JACK LAWRENCE
Colors by: ANDER ZARATE

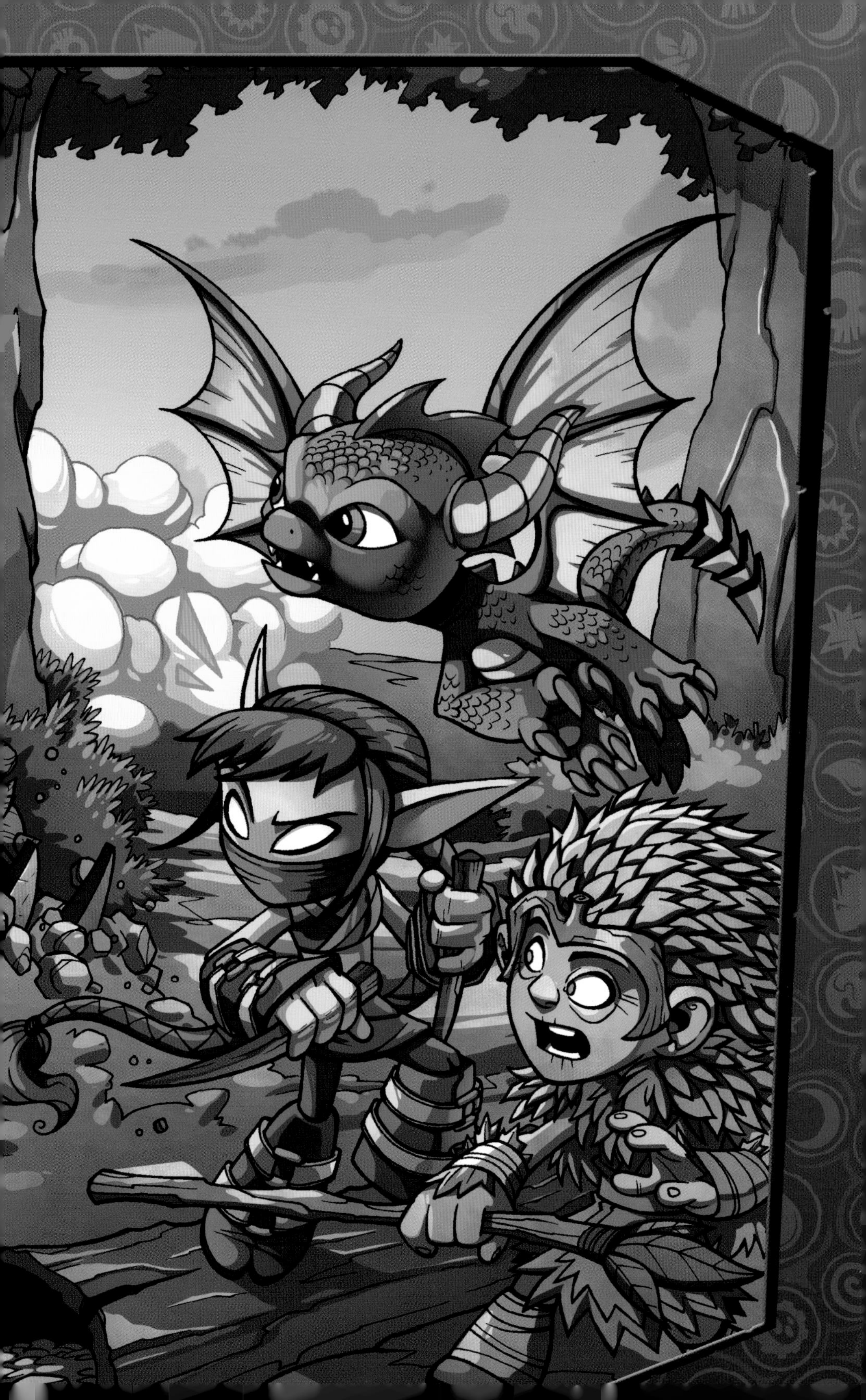

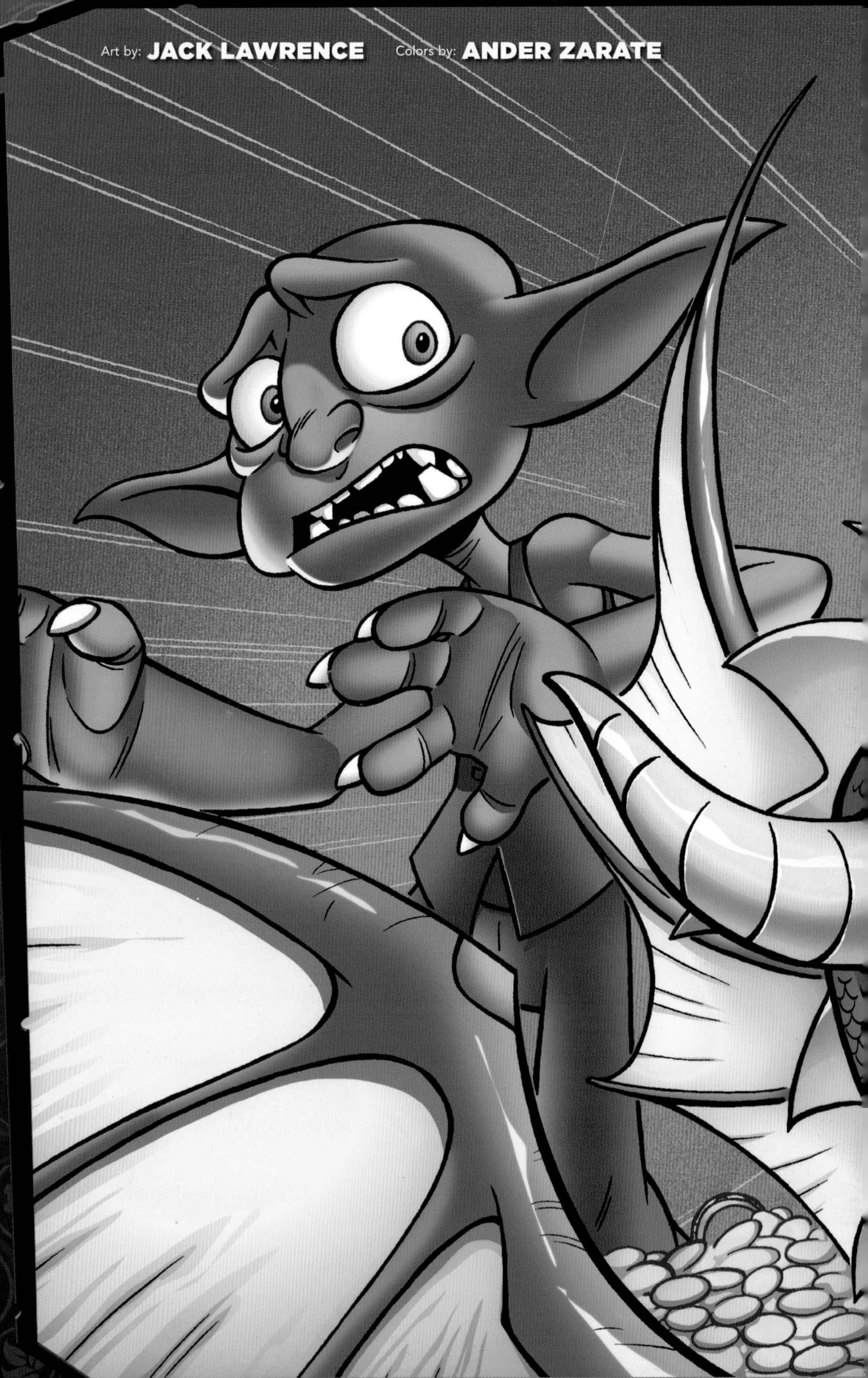
Art by: JACK LAWRENCE
Colors by: ANDER ZARATE

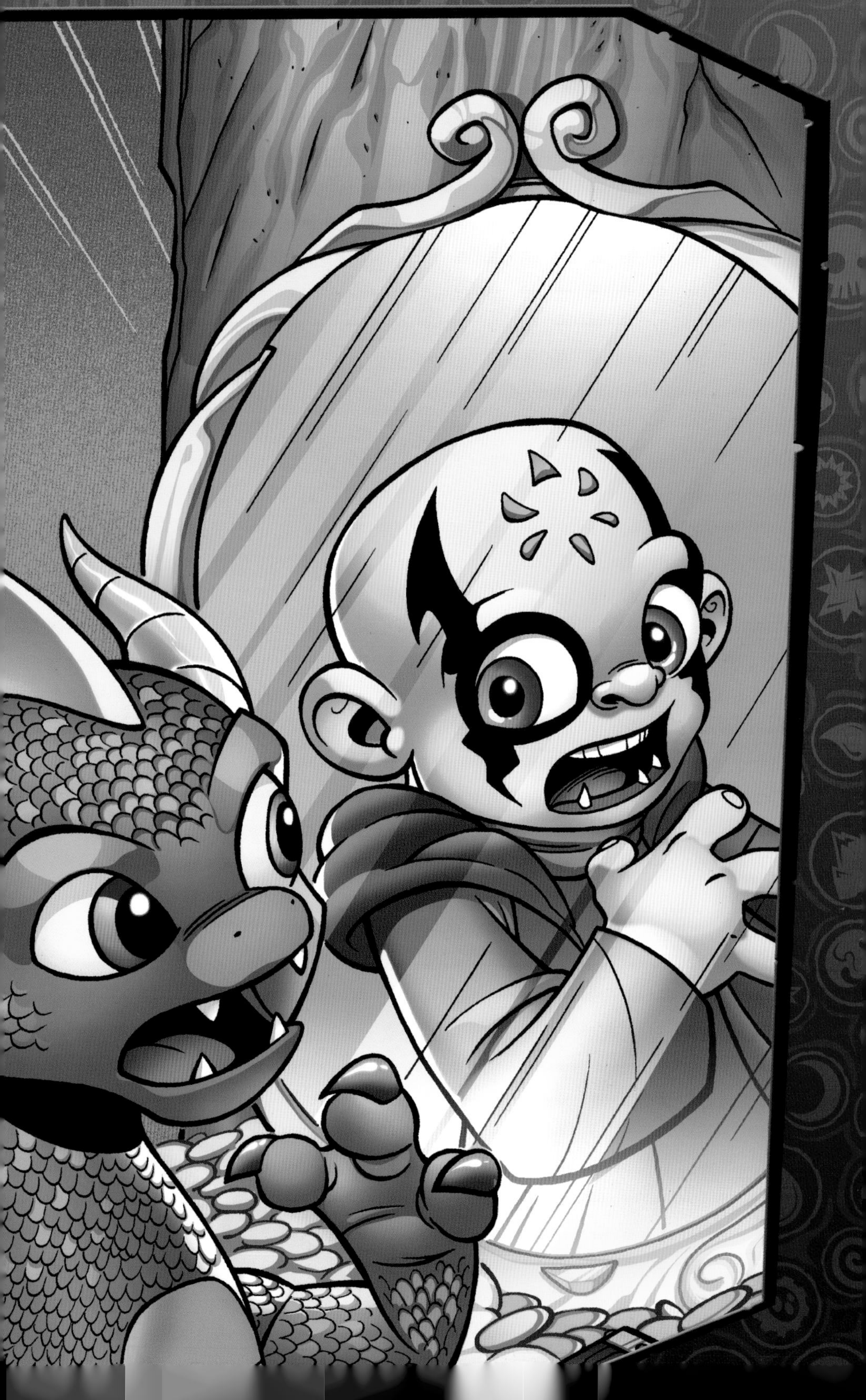

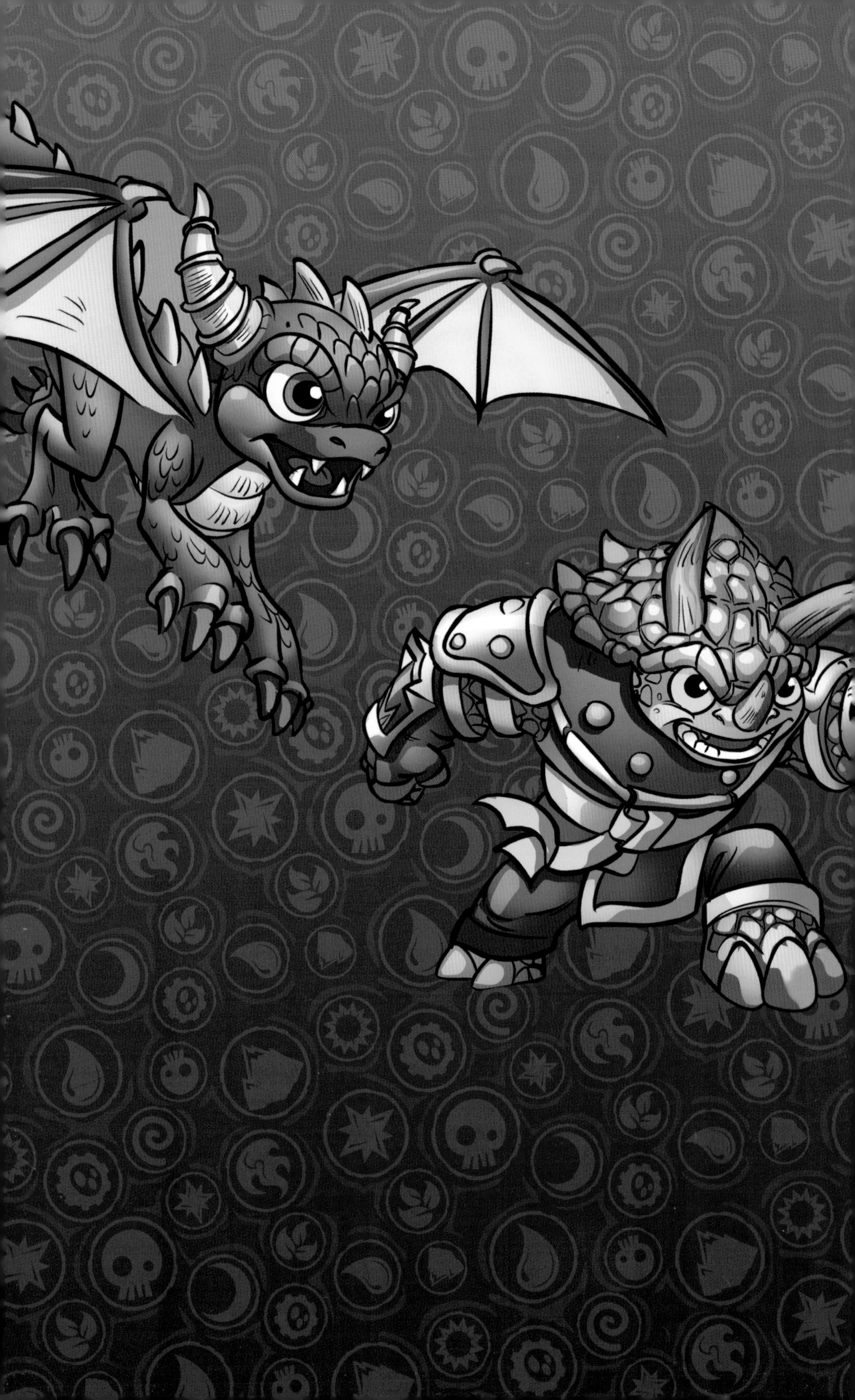